INTERLUDE

Book Two of the Stone Legacy Series

Theresa DaLayne

FOREWORD

From the moment I imagined Tara and Peter, I knew they would be special. Unfortunately, getting to know someone involves getting to know their past, and not everyone's past is peaches and cream. That goes for Tara as well. As revealed in *Mayan Blood*, Tara was a victim of childhood abuse. As a courtesy, I want to provide a *warning* to readers who have been victims of sexual abuse or childhood abuse because I've learned reading about such experiences can sometimes trigger unwanted memories or feelings.

While Tara has this in her past, there is absolutely no depiction of her time spent in the abusive environment where she was raised. However, the situation she finds herself in during this book could be upsetting to some.

Chapter One

Tara rested her head on Peter's chest while they lay in his bed, watching TV. She kicked the blanket off of her, and then sighed. She should be happy. She finally had a family of sorts—a boyfriend who would do anything for her, and a best friend who was more like a sister. But she wasn't happy, and she couldn't tell anyone.

Peter's bed was somehow more comfortable than hers, and he seemed to want her there. That didn't stop her from feeling terrible over waking him up—for the third time that week. Her plush bed looked inviting, but it was home to her horrible nightmares. At least she wished they were nightmares…

She used to find solace in Zanya, back in the orphanage, when they were all each other had. Funny how life had changed so much, so fast. Best friends, they spent their entire lives dreaming of a future outside of the orphanage's walls, only to be sucked into a reality that surpassed even *their* idea of insane.

Back then it was Zanya whose dreams were filled with terror.

They'd been taken from the orphanage to Renato's estate in Belize, where they'd experienced so much, and discovered Zanya's dreams were real. Then they traveled to Moscow. That's when things had gone from bad to terrible for Tara.

Her throat tightened. She curled her fingers around Peter's T-shirt. Half asleep and with the TV on, he didn't seem to notice.

She fought to stay awake out of fear of reliving her time spent with Sarian, the underworld general. The nightly reminders hadn't gone away. In fact, they had only gotten worse.

It was just like when she was a kid, before she was taken from her mother by child protective services. Then, the fear of another encounter with her mother's "boyfriends" had coiled around her in a paralyzing way, stalking her day and night.

Her eyelids grew heavy, and her muscles ached for just a few hours of sleep. Being close to Peter somehow made it all better, for the moment. He chased away her demons and made her forget.

Peter pushed one of her curls aside and placed a soft kiss behind her ear. "How are you feeling?" he said in a groggy whisper.

She shrugged. He nudged her shoulder with his chin and rested his lips on the curve of her neck. His breath teased her skin.

She smiled and cringed away. "Knock it off. You know I'm ticklish."

"Mmm." He trailed kisses down to her shoulder.

The tickling subsided, and Tara's eyes fluttered closed. Her lips parted, fingers tightening around the blankets underneath her.

The smell of fresh rain filled the air. God, she loved his scent. The first time Peter had stepped close to her at Renato's house, it had washed over her like a wave of relief. After that, she just couldn't stay away.

"You think you can get some sleep?" he whispered. "You need it."

Tara composed herself and nodded. Even though he didn't push the issue, a tiny piece of her wished he'd keep kissing her neck to see where it went—see if she felt comfortable, without committing to anything from the beginning. After all, it was *she* who didn't want to take the next step in their relationship. Peter, however, would never put her into a situation she didn't ask for. He loved her too much. It was the first time she had experienced that kind of commitment from anyone. There was no way she'd risk ruining it with sex.

Tara sat up, rubbing the tight muscles in her neck. Every nightmare threw her body into a more tense and agitated state. Her appetite was all but gone, her sense of humor dimmed, and since the flashbacks had become more vivid, she'd nearly lost the ability to smile.

Peter's hands replaced hers and worked around her shoulders, massaging the knots into submission. Warmth radiated from his fingertips and spread through her body, soothing the tension. His healing ability had come in handy more than once over the last few weeks.

She exhaled and melted into him. "Thanks." She glanced at the digital clock. It was almost four in the morning. Guilt tore at her. "I really have to stop coming in here every time a memory breaks through. I'm not five."

"No, what you really have to do is tell Marzena that you're remembering more."

Marzena, the group's dreamwalker, had helped Tara unlock the hidden door in her mind, allowing them to find the memories to locate Sarian. If only she could go back in time and block that door with concrete and chains to seal the memories inside...

"I won't do that," Tara said. "Not yet anyway. It's not that bad." Only bad enough to wake her in a cold sweat with her stomach knotted and muscles so tender she was achy for days. "Besides, she isn't even in Moscow, so it's not like she could do anything about it."

"She would come back if you needed her."

"Well, I don't." Not if that meant putting her issues on display. "She already reached into my head once. I don't need her doing it again."

Peter leaned forward and wrapped his arms around her. "Even if it'll help?" He kissed her temple. "Come on, Tara. You know you can't keep doing this."

He was right, but she couldn't admit it aloud. She had been so selfish, staggering to his bedroom, shaking like a leaf. Not exactly a romantic midnight rendezvous. "I'm sorry I keep dragging you into this."

If she could just leave him alone, at least one of them would get some rest and not feel like a zombie.

With her stomach in knots, she scooted to the side of the mattress and stared blankly at the wall.

Lights from the TV danced, casting shadows over the room.

"Whatever you're dealing with, I'm here for you." His voice was soft and comforting.

She swallowed down the urge to cry.

Zanya was still working to counter Sarian by travelling decades into the past with Renato, Arwan, Hawa, and Jayden, leaving Marzena, Tara, and Peter behind. Tara had tried to curb her bitterness about that, especially since she had nobody to channel it toward. It wasn't Zanya's choice to leave them. That's what she kept telling herself, anyway.

Tara rubbed her throbbing eyes. It was probably good that Marzena had gone back to Belize to manage the workers while they patched up the damage to Renato's house. It needed to be done before they all went back—if they went back. Renato's house had already become her home. Her heart ached at the memory of it under attack. And with Marzena gone, no one had to know Tara was steadily losing her mind. Again.

Peter grabbed the remote and flipped through the channels. "There's nothing on that's not in Russian."

She glanced at the screen. Had the actors been speaking Russian? Showed how much she'd been paying attention. He stopped on a news station with a woman speaking English in a heavy Russian accent. Behind her, emergency lights from police cars and ambulances flashed. Tara sighed and slumped her shoulders forward. "The news?"

"There's nothing else on." He lifted the remote. "You want me to just turn it off?"

She shook her head. "Nah. Leave it. At least it's in English." She tuned in for the first time.

"Officers responded to a call of a suspected gang clash outside of the Moscow Academy of Science. Authorities say a confrontation occurred between a student and an alleged gang member when the student's younger sister was forced into a gang-marked vehicle. The victim, who was wounded at the scene, was a freshman. Sadly, he died before the ambulance could respond, while the alleged attacker, who was also wounded, is now being treated at the Yakimanka Hospital where he is in critical condition."

Tara pushed the power button on the remote and the screen winked off. "I changed my mind. Even if it is in English, that's just depressing."

"Yeah. Seriously."

"Poor guy," she whispered, imagining the look of terror on the brother's face while his little sister was being dragged away. "I hope they get her back."

Peter moved to the far side of the bed. "Get who back?"

"The girl who was kidnapped."

"Yeah." His yawn deepened her guilt. "Come on." He patted the mattress. "Lie down next to me."

It was still dark out. If she left now, he could catch at least a few hours of sleep before the morning. She stood up and walked toward the door.

"Where are you going?"

She paused with her fingers wrapped around the handle. "I'm letting you get some rest. I'll be fine until morning."

Whether that would prove true or not, only time would tell.

Chapter Two

Rays of morning sunlight crept through the windows of Tara's hotel room. She was already awake, staring at the door. Harsh whispers echoed from the hall, paired with rushed footsteps on the carpeted floors. She flung the covers aside and hurried across the room. The knob rattled, followed by several sharp pounds. She flinched, then peered through the peephole before flipping the deadbolt aside and swinging open the door.

Renato rushed in with Hawa hanging limp in his arms.

"Oh my God! What happened?"

Renato laid her on the bed. Black hair spilled over Hawa's face as she moaned.

Peter stumbled into the room, his eyes glossy with sleep. Renato waved him in. "We need your help."

"Why didn't you come to my room?" Peter asked, rushing toward them.

"I…" Renato ran his fingers through his hair. "I was confused. I couldn't remember…"

Tara had never seen him like this before—

scattered and completely undone. Her chest tightened. "Where's Zanya?" Renato didn't say a word. Tara stepped forward. A knot formed in her gut. She gripped the bedpost, her legs beginning to feel like mush. "Mr. Renato, what happened to Zanya?"

"She'll be fine," Peter said while examining Hawa's bandaged leg. "I don't sense any breaks or fractures. But I think she may have a mild concussion." He stared up at Renato. "What the hell happened?"

Renato paced, rubbing the five o'clock shadow darkening his jaw line. "Sarian was much stronger than we anticipated. When Zanya tried to retrieve the stone, he somehow sensed her, even with the masking spell."

Figures. It was dangerous and stupid to accept the witch's offer to help. Tara had hated the idea from the start, but being outnumbered, and a girl with no abilities to contribute, she'd thought it better to keep her mouth shut. For all they knew, Contessa could have given Zanya a dud spell so she could take the stone herself. The witch only helped to get revenge on Sarian in the first place. It still wasn't clear how strong Zanya's stone really was, but since every underworlder wanted to get their hands on it, it had to be capable of some unworldly things.

And Zanya, as its guardian, was the only thing in their way.

"Who healed Hawa?" Peter asked.

"Contessa. At her home." Renato checked his watch. "We arrived in Moscow several hours ago."

"Besides a small concussion, it looks like she did a decent job." Peter laid the back of his hand against Hawa's forehead. "No fever. One or two healing sessions and I think she'll be back to normal. Right now she's exhausted. We should let her sleep."

Tara let go of the bedpost, anger peeling away her layers of patience. There was no way she'd let them keep ignoring her. With her fists perched on her hips, she narrowed her eyes. "If someone doesn't answer me in the next two seconds, I swear I'm going to flip the hell out." They both stopped and stared at her. Tara swallowed. "Where is Zanya?"

Renato gave a deep exhale. "Tara."

His calm, solemn tone sucked the heat right out of her body. It had to be bad.

She wound her fingers into her mess of red curls. "Oh no. What?"

"Please don't panic," he continued. "She is not hurt."

Tara exhaled. "Thank God." She swallowed down the spike of anxiety. "Don't scare me like that." She gestured toward the hall. "I'm gonna go talk to her." When she started toward the door, Renato stepped into her path. She examined his tight features. "I'll be right back," she said. "I just want to go see how she's holding up."

"Tara." When he said her name the second time his tone hadn't change, and the look in his eyes told her something was wrong. He ran his hands down the length of his jacket, smoothing it down. "She's not here."

"What do you mean she's not here? You said

she's all right."

"Yes, that's true."

Tara shifted her weight. "Well, where is she?"

"She and Arwan left to get Jayden back."

"Back?" Tara scanned the room. In the chaos, she hadn't noticed the absence of Jayden or Arwan. "Is Jay pulling another stunt to try and win Zanya over?"

"I don't think that's what's going on this time," Peter said.

"Sarian is stronger than we realized."

Her heart pounded faster. "But..." Tara's gaze darted between them. "I don't understand."

Renato rested his hand on her shoulder. "Tara...Jayden was killed in battle."

It was as if someone had kicked her in the stomach. She wheezed and gripped her belly. "What?" Her bottom lip quivered along with her voice. She had known Jayden nearly as long as Zanya. Even if they weren't as close, he was a dear friend. She swallowed past the ache in her throat.

Peter took her hand.

"Zanya and Arwan have rushed to Guatemala," Renato continued. "To the caves of Naj Tunich."

She tightened her grip around Peter's hand while suspicion crawled over her. "Zanya hates caves. Especially after her run-in with that demon thing Sarian sent. Why would she want to go there?"

"I attempted to convince her it was a dangerous, reckless idea, but she insisted. She was determined. She and Arwan have traveled to the caves to find Houn—the Guardian of Souls. She has the insane plan to get Jayden's soul back and resurrect him."

Tara pulled away from Peter, grabbed Renato's collar, and jerked him forward. "Are you trying to tell me that my best friend is going to meet up with the Grim Reaper?"

Renato stared down at Tara's fingers clenching his coat.

She let go and stepped back. "No. Zanya wouldn't just take off like that. Not without telling me first."

Renato straightened his posture, smoothing the wrinkles in his clothes. "I managed to rent a cold chamber for Jayden's body in the local morgue."

Tara snorted. "Yeah, I think you're full of it." No way this could be real.

His lips formed a tight line. "If escorting you to see his body is the only way to convince you I am being honest, that is certainly an option."

Tara's eyes widened. "You're not joking."

"Unfortunately, no. If Zanya and Arwan cannot retrieve his soul before Houn places it in the underworld, the morgue is where Jayden's body belongs. Either way, we need to preserve it the best we can."

"Preserve?" She choked on the word and slowly sat beside Hawa on the mattress.

"Something has been bothering me since we left Moscow," Renato said, staring into the distance. "Why would Houn hold his soul when Jayden died in battle? Why would he not go straight to the heavens?"

"It would have…unless there's a good reason he's there," Peter said.

Renato nodded. "Unless *someone* wanted him

there."

Tara cupped her hand over her mouth. Was this another trap for Zanya?

Peter rested his hand on her shoulder. "It'll be all right."

She wanted to believe him, but something in her gut told her it wouldn't be that simple. "Jayden's dead and…Zanya didn't even say goodbye. What if—" Her breath caught. "What if I never see her again?"

***

Chills ran over Tara's body, her clothes soaked in sweat. She peeled open her eyes to blurry vision and a low ache throbbing through her temples.

The muscles in her shoulders screamed when she tilted her head back to watch tiny rays of light push through rusted bars set high in the rock walls—the only light in the otherwise dark space.

If she had to guess by the scent of musty earth, and the tree roots pushing through the dirt beneath her feet, she was underground in some sort of dungeon.

She wrinkled her nose at another scent— metallic, like…copper.

When she tried to move, a searing wall of pain shot up her legs. Her scream echoed through the lonely space.

The spike of agony dulled enough for her to wearily look down at the wooden boards squeezing her legs. A rope bound her limbs together, and wooden wedges were between her knees. She quickly deflected her gaze, too terrified to see how bad her injuries really were.

Memories of the boards, rope, and heavy iron mallet flooded her mind. Worse was the pain as the splints slowly bowed her bones.

Something textured slithered over her bare feet, the sensation faint against her numb toes. They used to hurt—now she couldn't decide if the lack of pain was good or bad. With her hands tied behind the back of the chair, she couldn't lean forward to see what was moving beneath her.

She examined the stone ceiling. Tiny pools of condensation collected and dripped, creating a symphony of tiny sounds that echoed in the silence.

Something else brushed against her ankle. This time the rough texture was clear as it scraped against her skin. Peeking over the front of the chair the best she could, she searched the ground.

"Please don't let it be a rat," she whispered.

Rats would eat anything, and she could very well be on its dinner menu.

Footsteps carried through the hollow space. The rusted keyhole clicked open, and the heavy iron door shuddered in the stone wall.

He had returned for another round of torture.

She shook her head. Blood-soaked hair stuck to her neck and forehead. She shut her eyes, her head throbbing enough to remind her a piece of her scalp had been cut off right after she was taken.

"Please..." The word croaked out of her tight throat. "Please, just leave me alone."

Against her request, hinges screamed with age as the door creaked open.

Sobs from neighboring cells filled the air.
All that awaited her was terror and death.

***

Tara gasped and sat up in bed. Her eyes, her head—hell, just about every part of her body hurt one way or another.

She stumbled to the bathroom and turned on the faucet. A few splashes of cold water over her face didn't help to slow heart stomping in her chest. Unable to consider going back to sleep, she wearily dragged herself back into her room and into the closet to change.

She'd woken Peter three times in the past week with her nightmares. So instead of dragging him into her world of unbearable fatigue, she would suffer this night alone.

Maybe if she had some kind of ability like the others, she'd be strong enough to block out the memories, or at least not allow them to affect her so much. Instead, she'd become a groupie—and a useless one at that. The reality of being worthless tore at her. She had dealt with that emotion enough after she was taken from her mom.

Those early years were still so vivid in her mind, watching as her mother stumbled through the front door, waking her out of a deep sleep. Most nights Tara changed into her pajamas alone, brushed her own teeth, and tucked herself in. On rare occasions, her mom might be there—sober—and would kiss her goodnight. Usually, Tara would get just a glance and a few mumbles from her mom as she told the new boyfriend to ignore her kid. One night, a man followed her mom into the bedroom, staring at Tara over his shoulder.

He may have been the first one to touch her, but he wouldn't be the last.

Tara's stomach clenched. She needed some fresh air.

Out of the hotel and into the city of Moscow, Tara wandered the streets. Bars overflowed with people sipping colorful drinks. Music thumped through the windows. Neon signs flashed over tavern doors. The aroma of alcohol and tobacco mixed with the aroma of street food made her mouth water.

She swallowed down the saliva pooled under her tongue and stared longingly at the food cart. Why wouldn't she be hungry after not eating for a day…or two? She couldn't remember exactly how long it had been since she had a proper meal.

A stop at a street cart landed her with a stuffed baked potato wrapped in tinfoil. She found a step to sit on, and began picking at the food with a plastic fork.

Her stomach rolled as she scooped up a cheesy bite. Ketchup glazed the top of the loaded spud, and it looked like carnage. Her hunger pains vanished, replaced with the sudden urge to vomit. "Damn it."

A stray dog sniffed around the sidewalk—the perfect scapegoat for her unwanted meal. With a wagging tail and pinned back ears, it inched toward her. She stood and held out her dinner. "Are you hungry?" The spotted hound sniffed the air, its nose leading it closer. After a moment of hesitation, it grabbed Tara's offering and wolfed it down in a few quick bites. She smiled lightly, balling the wrapper in her hands. "At least *you* got to eat something." Her mind swirled into a haze, and she clung to the railing for support. The buildings spun like a carousel from hell.

She'd have to force herself to eat soon. Her body couldn't take much more neglect.

"You shouldn't feed strays."

Tara jumped and spun to see a man sitting on the step above her. The heavy door behind him was tagged with graffiti. She hadn't heard it open—or maybe she just hadn't noticed with the tornado in her head.

"How long have you been sitting there?"

She peered into his face, his eyes hidden behind dark rings of black makeup, like he'd gone way overboard on eyeliner.

He shrugged. "Not long."

Tara cringed. This dude was bad news. Bad vibes. Bad everything. Whether she was uneasy because she couldn't see him clearly in the dark, or because the guy looked like some emo-goth hybrid, or because he'd completely snuck up on her, she wasn't sure. One thing *was* for sure. She wouldn't stick around to find out why he was talking to her.

She stood and walked away from the steps, her head down and her sneakers moving at a rhythmic pace over the sidewalk. When she glanced over her shoulder, he was gone. She slowed her pace to a stop, searching the empty step. "What the hell?"

She turned around and sucked in a sharp breath. He stood in front of her—the same guy who had been sitting *behind* her a second ago.

The cherry of his cigarette cast a subtle red light over his face. "What are you doing out here alone?"

Tara took a cautious backward step. "Just going for a walk."

"Couldn't sleep?"

He could be a murderer or rapist. He could be the damn BTK killer for all she knew, and he was staring right at her. Maybe going for a stroll in the middle of the night wasn't the best idea after all.

People paraded the streets, most of them drunk and belligerent.

He tilted his head to the side.

Tara pointed over her shoulder with her thumb, taking more backward steps. "I'm just going to...go." When he didn't reply, she turned and walked briskly in the opposite direction.

After a few minutes, she spotted the hotel doors ahead. The fact she was about to wake Peter made her feel like the world's worst girlfriend, but after her run-in with creepy Goth guy, she didn't want to be alone. She walked inside and headed up the elevator to their floor.

After a gentle knock, Peter's door creaked open and sleepy blue eyes blinked out at her. "What's wrong?" His voice was raspy, deepening her guilt.

Tara shrugged. "Couldn't sleep. Went for a walk."

He opened the door all the way. With no shirt, his low riding shorts showcased his lean, chiseled torso. Tara bit her lip.

"Come on in." She moved into his room, and he closed the door behind her. She did her best to ignore the frown pulling at the corners of his mouth. "What do you mean you went for a walk? It's almost four in the morning."

"Yeah. I know." She peeled off her coat and draped it over his messy bed before she sat.

He rested beside her. "Another memory?"

She hung her head, giving no reply. There was nothing to say, really. Telling him about it would only make him worry more.

"You promised me you'd tell Renato if this got worse." His tone turned from concerned to upset. He rested his hand on her leg. "Tara—"

"Just…" She sighed and reached out, finding bare skin, muscle, and warmth. She spread her fingers over his chest.

"Do you want to sleep here tonight?"

She bit her lip. "Umm…"

He stood and walked to his suitcase pushed against the far wall. He dug out a cotton shirt and rested it on the bed beside her.

She picked it up. The material was warm and soft between her cold fingers. She glanced at him, offering the best smile she could. "You'll eventually get sick of me wearing your clothes."

He winked. "I highly doubt that."

Staying the night seemed unfair, but the offer was too tempting to turn down. Plus, all of her pajamas were dirty. She'd been going through them faster than she could wash them. Somehow, sweat soaked pajamas weren't quite as appealing to sleep in.

She locked herself in the bathroom and pulled his T-shirt over her thinning frame. The seam ended just below her thighs. She came out to find Peter re-making the bed. He pulled down a corner of the sheets for her to climb in. "I'm gonna sleep on the floor."

With all of the trouble he'd gone through, she couldn't say no. "Are you sure? I can sleep on the floor."

He huffed with a grin. "Not happening. But I *am* stealing one of these." He threw a feather pillow on a thin blanket he'd spread over the carpet.

She slipped under the cool, dry linens. He kissed her forehead, and then lay down on the floor beside her. With her cheek cradled on the pillow, she inhaled the scent of freshly fallen rain.

For long moments she fought the deep exhaustion settled in her bones. It taunted and beckoned to her. She clung to her pillow, her eyes closing without her permission. When her mind wandered into that quiet space, she sucked in a shallow breath and opened her eyes again, now burning for rest.

Peter pushed up on his elbows, his face half hidden in the shadows. "You can't keep going on like this."

A tear ran down her cheek and dampened the pillowcase. "I know."

CHAPTER THREE

Tara sighed and pushed her spoon around the steaming bowl of oatmeal topped with pecans, raisins, and a splash of brown sugar. It smelled so good. Her stomach tightened and slithered. If she could just eat a few bites…

She loaded the spoon and brought it to her lips. The aroma rose and teased her senses, but when the oatmeal touched her tongue, the back of her throat tightened, and she nearly gagged.

She noticed Renato watching her, and quickly dropped the spoon back in her bowl.

"You look like shit," Hawa said.

Peter huffed. "So typical for you to say something like that."

Hawa shrugged and spooned another bite into her mouth while grinning.

Tara glared. Maybe Hawa thought she was stupid, or naive. She certainly wasn't blind. Anyone could see how Hawa masked her feelings for Peter with her "I don't give a shit about anything" attitude. It was getting old. Fast. After a week of not sleeping, Tara wasn't in the mood to put up with any of Hawa's crap.

Renato cleared his throat and sipped his coffee. "You are looking a bit tired. Is everything all right?"

"I'm fine, just…stressed. Worried, about Zanya." She tucked a curl behind her ear. "You haven't heard from her?"

"Not yet, but I'm sure they're well."

"Or dead." Hawa finished the last bite of her oatmeal and dropped the spoon in her bowl. It clattered against the ceramic before settling on the edge.

Tara's fingers tightened around the corner of the table. "What the hell is your problem?"

Hawa's eyebrow arched. "Oh, so she has a voice."

"Why are you so damn bitter? If it's because of Peter, you need to just get over it. You aren't going to win him back, especially with the whole 'bad ass' act. You think you're fooling everyone, but you're not. Get a grip, and move on."

Everyone sat silent as Tara pushed out of her chair. Hawa glared with rigid shoulders. Tara waited to see if the little brat had anything else to add. She wanted Hawa to say something, hoped she would, so Tara could vent more of her frustration.

Tara glanced at Renato and found his expression drenched in disappointment. Even Peter picked at his oatmeal without even look at her.

Her cheeks swelled with heat.

She left the table and barged into the hall, down to the lobby, and out the front doors. With her fists clenched, she stalked down the sidewalk. "Who the hell does she think she is, anyway?"

"Tara." She continued walking, even after hearing Peter call her name. "Tara, wait up!" The pounding of his sneakers grew louder until they slowed, and he fell into pace beside her. "What was that all about?"

She couldn't bear to look at him. "What? Was I too hard on her?"

He grabbed her hand and pulled her to a stop. She finally met his gaze. "You know I don't think of her like that anymore."

"Then why don't you tell her to just get over you?"

He rubbed the back of his neck with his free hand. "I mean, I guess I just assumed she would, after enough time passed. I might not like her like *that*, but I don't want to hurt her feelings either."

Tara jerked her hand away from his. "Well, she obviously hasn't gotten the clue, and since you're too nice to tell her to back off, I had to."

"You're not acting like yourself. These memories are really wearing you down. You need to talk to Renato."

"I'm sure you would just love for me to be the walking freak show. Someone you need to take care of." She spun and continued down the sidewalk, Peter on her heels. "I'm nobody's charity case. Ever since I was a kid, people have felt sorry for me. That's not my life anymore, and I'm trying not to relive it *every single day*, thanks."

"You're not a charity case, Tara. You never have been."

"Then stop treating me like it!"

"I'm treating you like someone I care about. Your body can't take much more of this. I can sense it when I touch you. Your energy is weakening."

She snorted. "I've only been awake for like, oh, a week straight. I haven't been able to eat because everything makes me want to puke. I'm light headed, exhausted, and—"

"Tara." He took her hand and pulled her to a stop again, this time with a gentle caress. His tenderness slowed her boiling rage. "I love you, and I just want you to be happy and healthy."

His fingers worked through her curls. He pressed his warm lips to her forehead and lingered there. The scent of fresh rain flowed around them, this time with a hint of sweet wildflowers.

She leaned into him, her heart aching. "I just want to be myself again."

"Come on." He began to lead her back to the hotel. "I'll go with you to talk to him."

She dug her heels into the pavement. Apparently he wasn't getting the point. She didn't want to be too pushy, but he needed to understand. "I told you, I'm not going."

"You need help, Tara."

She crossed her arms. "If I tell him…he won't say it, but…" She hung her head. "He won't want me around anymore if he thinks I'm messed up."

"How could you say that? Renato cares about you."

"He doesn't even know me." She bit the inside of her cheek. "Not really. And I'm not like you guys. I'm just dead weight."

He cupped her face in his hands. "That is *not*

true."

Tears stung her eyes. He didn't deserve this crap. She pulled away from him. "I'm going for a walk. Alone."

***

Tara sat on the patio of a quaint diner beneath strokes of orange and red in the twilight sky, sipping a club soda. Although bitter, the carbonation curbed her appetite, and she needed something—anything—to make her stomach stop the rotation of growling, aching, and then nausea.

She'd been watching the locals all afternoon. It was fascinating to see how people acted outside of some sterile institution like her orphanage. Aside from the locals, tons of tourists passed through the streets, offering plenty of variety.

A black sedan sat idle on the opposite side of the street. The driver—a man with a dark goatee and wearing a black *ushanka*—tapped his fingers on the steering wheel to a beat.

He appeared to be a native Russian, the kind who was born and raised in the country and would never leave. She must have been staring too long because the driver noticed her. For a split second, they locked eyes. She quickly averted her gaze to the ceramic ashtray in the center of her table.

Maybe he hadn't realized she was watching him, specifically. If she focused somewhere else long enough, he might forget and go back to tapping his fingers to his music.

Her muscles jammed up when her peripheral

vision caught him stepping out of the car. She'd been sitting there most of the afternoon, and nobody had noticed her until now. She shifted in her chair as he approached.

Her eyes slowly scaled his body when he came to a stop in front of her table, looking like some kind of military commander in a heavy wool jacket over a pair of jeans tucked into combat boots, and a wool hat lined with fur.

"May I sit?" A heavy Russian accent thickened his words. Tara swallowed and nodded. It went against her better judgment, but she didn't have it in her to say no.

He pulled out a chair. Rows of heavy rings decorated his fingers. His gaze bore into her while she struggled not to seem obviously uncomfortable. She had no idea what to say or do, so she sat there frozen, hoping he would just go away.

"I saw you watching me. Are you wanting something?"

Tara shook her head.

He examined her for a long moment. "Are you sure?" He leaned forward, his forearms propped on the table. Hidden under his hand was a Ziploc bag with two pills. "Very good. Pure."

Tara's body heat spiked. Someone had to be watching, and had to have noticed this guy offering her drugs.

She shook her head again. "I don't need anything, thanks." Her voice came out as a squeak.

"This is what many say. But..." He slid the baggie across the table and dropped the cloth napkin on top of it. "This is for no charge." He placed a business card on the table in front of her with only two words written across the navy blue background—*Club Grunge.*

Before she could muster up the courage to object, he stood and walked away, leaving her alone with the baggie and two tiny pink pills inside. Even under the cover of the napkin, the drugs seemed to be screaming for attention from every cop in a ten-block radius. She sat like a statue, staring at the cloth.

Her waiter strolled to her table with a tray in his hand. "Would you like your check?"

It was probably a good idea to get out of there. She slumped back in her chair and nodded.

"Let me get these things out of your way." When he reached for the empty bottle of S.Pellegrino and napkin, her heart nearly exploded.

She pounced her hands over the hidden baggie and froze. The waiter pulled back and stared at her with wide eyes.

"I…I'm actually not done yet." She flashed a tight-lipped smile. "Sorry. Give me, uh…give me another bottle of this stuff." She tapped the glass bottle. "Please."

With raised eyebrows, he said nothing, and turned and walked away. She grabbed the baggie and business card and shoved them into her pocket. She would throw the pills away somewhere, and nobody would be the wiser. Her muscles began to relax.

That was it. She'd just throw them away.

Everything would be fine.

Nobody would ever know.

After dropping some money on the table, Tara left the restaurant. Quick steps brought her closer to an alley with a trashcan on the corner. She reached into her pocket and curled her fingers around pills. All she wanted was to be rid of it, and get back to Peter, who was probably worried about her. She'd acted like such a jerk.

"Hey, trouble."

Tara glanced over her shoulder at a pair of eyes lined in black. "What the hell?" She turned to face him. "Are you stalking me?"

"I could ask the same question." He lit a cigarette.

She crinkled her nose at the stench of burning earth and chemicals whirling in the air. "The answer would be no."

He gestured to her jacket pocket with a nod of his head. "You going to take those?"

"Take what?" She tightened her hold around the baggie.

"Andrei isn't the kind of guy you want to screw around with. Trust me. He hangs around some not so normal people."

"How do you know his name?" She glanced down the street at the black sedan, then turned her attention back to the weirdo in front of her. "And what about you? If I've acquired my own personal stalker, I should at least know what to call you."

He paused for a moment, and one side of his mouth curled into a grin. "Malachi."

She crossed her arms. "Okay, Malachi. So why are you following me around?"

He took another drag from his cigarette. His skin

was as white as the smoke snaking from his lips. "You interest me."

"Well, that's not creepy." Tara turned and walked away, hoping he wouldn't follow.

No such luck.

"Where are you going?"

His stare bore into her back. Her skin crawled. "Why do you care?" She kept her head down and increased her pace, her goal set on the hotel just ahead.

"Never know." His voice became more distant as the space between them grew. "Someday you might need me."

"I highly doubt that." Another glance over her shoulder stopped her dead in her tracks. Standing at the foot of the hotel steps, she searched the sidewalk and found pedestrians in heavy coats and tourists carrying cameras, but no Malachi.

CHAPTER FOUR

Tara's mother strolled into the cell—Sarian, cloaked in yet another form. Her strawberry blonde hair—thinning from age and the constant abuse of cocaine and tequila—fell straight over her shoulders.

She looked exactly like Tara remembered from the last time they saw each other, when Tara was just five. She probably wouldn't remember her mother at all if it weren't for the few photos she had at the orphanage. Now that they were gone too, her memory had started to fade, and her mother's face had become a blurred image she struggled to see.

Until now.

Tara had managed to stay composed through Sarian's prior attempts to tear information out of her, but she couldn't tell what she didn't know. Of course, Sarian didn't believe her. Still, this time, in the form of her mother, Tara's heart shriveled, and after a moment of watching the woman, Tara turned her head.

Drops of cold sweat zigzagged down her back and over the ridges of her spine.

"Where is your guardian when you need her?" Her mother whispered in a soft coo.

Tara's bottom lip quivered. "Please...let me go."

"And if I do, will you tell me how to break the obedience spell?" With a delicate touch, she lifted Tara's chin, forcing her to look into her mother's eyes. The same brown, tired eyes Tara had stared into as a child, hoping her mother was sober enough to sing Twinkle, Twinkle Little Star *before bed. The same eyes that returned her childlike hope with sharp glares of resentment. Her mother had never wanted her. That much had always been clear.*

Anger churned inside her. Sarian had approached her in the form of Renato and Zanya, but this was an all-time low. She wouldn't give him the satisfaction of seeing her fall apart.

From under the folds of her baggy sweatshirt, her mother withdrew a heavy mallet. Tara gasped and tried to shake free, but the splints clamped around her legs kept her from trying more than once. Pain quaked up her body, blurring her vision.

"Usually, the Boots are very effective in extracting information—a method from the medieval era." Her mother's lips curled into an insidious grin. She held up the mallet, slowly rotating in front of Tara's face. "But perhaps I should try another approach." She lowered the weapon, and her figure morphed until the mallet transformed into a cane. Her mother's body morphed into Sarian's—her mother's baggy sweats changed into his sharp suit and her brown, resentful

eyes grew dark, almost black. He leaned on his cane, his hair slicked back. "Perhaps I'll allow Yaxche to have its way with you instead." His voice had returned to his own, though that wasn't any comfort.

A slithering root caught her peripheral vision. Tara frantically glanced around. Thick coil snaked up from the soil and over the ground beneath her feet.

"This tree has kept the dead trapped in the underworld since time began." Sarian slowly backed away.

The chair cradling her body began to tremble. Tiny vines sprouted from the armrests and crawled along her wrist. Her breath stalled when she realized that the entire time she'd been bound, her chair had been roots from the world tree, all woven together and perfectly still.

The prison cell door slammed shut, and Sarian peered through the bars. "I'm sure it would appreciate a live meal. That is, unless you have some information for me."

Vines wound around her feet. Thicker roots sprouted around the edge of the room, scarlet capillaries clustering under the bark. The writhing vines caressed the delicate skin on the back of her hand. They moved with the rhythm of her chest, rising and falling with every breath. Paralyzed with fear, she could only sit there in horror as she realized...

The roots were breathing.

***

Shaky, Tara managed to make it to the bathroom before her knees buckled. She grabbed onto the sink for support and splashed cold water on her face. Drops slid down her nose and chin as she stared in the mirror at the ghostly reminisce of her former self.

A small part of her wished she'd had an answer to Sarian's question. She hadn't known anything about the obedience spell at the time. Hell, she still didn't. No details at least. If she had, she could have told him, and it all would have ended. It wouldn't have been a total loss. He eventually figured it out anyway, from what had Peter said.

She wouldn't know firsthand.

Tara hadn't seen Zanya since it happened, and the knowledge her best friend was out there, fighting to save Jayden without complete control of her stone, made Tara's stomach ache. Knowing her friend's life was at risk, she couldn't have told Sarian. Not if it meant she would be responsible for the consequences: the blood of countless innocent people on her hands. No thanks.

She peered closer into her reflection. The shadows under her eyes were darker than before. Even her curls were droopy and sad.

Tara paused, wondering what else about her had changed.

She hesitantly stepped in front of the full-length mirror and peeled off her pajamas. Standing in her underwear, the full gravity of her deterioration was in clear view. Her ribs were defined, and her pelvic bones had begun to protrude. She had always wanted to be thinner, to smooth out her curves until she had a lean torso and slim hips—but not this way.

She walked out of the bathroom, leaving her PJ's on the floor. They smelled of sweat and fear.

Back in bed, she hugged a pillow against her chest and rested her cheek against the soft linen. There was no way she could go back to sleep now. That last flashback was enough to keep her awake for weeks. She could still feel the vines tightening around her wrists, and hear the slow, hissing exhale of the tree.

This must be what Zanya had endured all those nights in the orphanage—the reason she never slept, and hated the night and the dark. She understood now.

The down feather pillow held the aroma of fabric softener. Not even a hint of fresh rain or sweet wildflowers. With a deep sigh, she crawled out from between the sheets and slipped on her robe, then cracked the door open and peeked into the silent hall.

The soft glow of the evening lights cast warmth across the hotel walls. Quiet steps led her to Peter's door. She knocked, her heart growing heavy while she waited for him to answer in the middle of the night for the umpteenth time. It wasn't right for her to drag him into her mess. She still hadn't apologized for the way she took her frustration out on him earlier that day. Without Peter, she would be all alone. He was the only comfort she had now that Zanya was gone.

Dark fog clouded the edges of her vision. *Damn dizzy spells.* Tara rested her palm on the wall to ground herself.

The door opened, and Tara quickly stood up straight. She didn't want to worry him, although it was obvious by the look on his face that her effort hadn't paid off. Peter stepped aside with the door open, inviting her in.

The scent of fresh rain soothed her as she entered his room. His fingers caught her wrist, and she melted into him.

He deserved so much better than her.

"I'm sorry," she whispered.

He pushed the door shut and wrapped his arms around her. "Don't ever be sorry for needing me. I'm always here."

She sniffled, her entire body aching for relief. She curled her fingers through his shaggy hair and trailed her hands down his shoulders. "Mmm, you smell so good." Her lips found the curve under his jaw. He tasted just as amazing.

A soft laugh bubbled from his chest. "Do I?" His hands found her waist and ran up the soft robe, over the curves of her back.

The more she realized how safe he made her feel, the more she wanted to be close to him. She wanted to be submerged in his serenity, his flavor, his skin.

Suddenly the answer to her turmoil became clear.

She brushed her lips over his and untied the belt of her robe. When she shrugged her shoulders back, the robe slipped off and puddled onto the floor, leaving her standing in her underwear.

His skin was warm under her fingers. She

pressed her body closer to his.

Peter's muscles flexed beneath her palms. A hint of guilt made her hesitate. She'd told him when they first started dating that she wasn't ready for this, and ever since, she'd held true to that oath. Her advances were going against everything they'd established, but she couldn't help herself. She needed him to take away the pain.

Her heart fluttered with each breath. He tasted like heaven, or the first rays of sunlight breaking through the night sky. Tara whimpered and opened her mouth just enough for his tongue to slip between her lips.

Peter didn't disappoint. He gripped her hips, sending a shiver over her skin.

He broke away, spent a moment gazing into her eyes, and smiled. She laced her fingers between his and led him toward the bed.

"You came here for this?" His voice sounded deeper, softer, and more seductive than ever heard before.

There was no reason to reply. He may not know *why* she wanted him, but it was obvious *what* she wanted. When they reached the bed, Tara's turned to face him. This would be the first time she would willingly give herself to anyone. If she thought about it too much, she'd lose her nerve.

Peter followed her onto the plush mattress. One hand planted on either side of her, he trapped her against the pillow. He let out a sharp breath when she pulled him closer.

Every touch melted away a bit of her misery and made it easier to forget. His solid body pushed against hers, and she sucked in a tiny gasp.

His lips found hers again, but he all too quickly pulled away. "I love you, Tara. You know that, don't you?"

Her heart swelled. She loved him too—more than even she could admit. He was the only one who could take away her suffering and soothe the torment torturing her body and heart.

She loved him, but as much as she hated to admit it, she *did* need him to fix her—or she might go insane.

Tara peered through the dark room as he backed away and climbed off the bed. He turned to a chair and began searching in his duffle bag, probably for protection. He must have been carrying it around. A mixture of fear and excitement whirled through her.

He came back with something in his hand, but it wasn't flat and square with a round bulge in a metallic wrapper.

It was black and velvet.

A box.

He flipped on the light, assaulting Tara's eyes. She blinked and found Peter lowering to one knee.

His hand quaked as he stared up at her. She hadn't seen him so nervous since the first time he kissed her.

The light in his eyes was so genuine. It should have made her happy.

Instead, her mind whitewashed with panic.

A ring?

She didn't want to jump to conclusions. Maybe it was just a pair of earrings, or a necklace. She'd feel like a total idiot if she freaked out before knowing for sure.

But if it was…Tara's muscles tensed.

He took her hand and kissed her knuckles. "First, I need to ask you something."

Tara dragged her legs over the side of the bed and gripped the edge of the mattress. "What is this, Peter?"

He drew in a deep breath. "You are the most amazing person I've ever met, and the days I spent not knowing if you were alive or dead were the worst days of my life. After that, I made a promise to myself that I would never let you go." He slowly opened the box to reveal a gold band with a pear cut diamond in the center, and tiny blue gems framing its sparkling curves.

She pressed her shaking fingers over her lips. This was bad. How could he ask her to marry him when she was…her, and he deserved so much more?

He shifted his weight, still on one knee. "Please, say something."

"Why are you asking me this now?" Now, when a part of her was using him for the peace he could give her.

He trailed his hand up her leg and rested it on her knee. "I know we're young, and it may seem crazy to everyone else, but I don't care. I want to be with you, but only if you love me enough to not regret it."

"Regret it?" Her throat went so dry.

"I want us to be together, Tara. I want *you*, forever."

Her limbs froze. "Forever?" Her mind exploded

with a sickening realization—one she'd never faced. Not until now. "Forever is a long time, Peter."

His lips parted, and he hung his head. "If you're going to say no, please…don't drag it out."

"I just…" It was as if someone had stabbed her in the chest. "Shit."

He stared up at her with parted lips. "That's the response I get? *Shit*?"

Her breath recoiled. "No. I'm sorry." She rubbed her eyes. "But…forever for you isn't forever for me." Despair filled her beyond capacity. "Haven't you ever thought about that?"

"What are you talking about?"

She admired the polished gold band and sparkling stones. "I'm not like you. Someday I'll leave you behind."

Peter pushed off the floor and sat beside her. "Don't think about that. You're all I want, and if we're going to be together like this…" His fingers trailed down the curve of her bare shoulder. "I want to be sure our first time isn't something you wish you could take back."

Slowly, her eyes met his, and a scar deep inside her heart tore open. A scar created from all the first times she had never wanted. All the first times her mom's boyfriends forced on her when she was too young to fight back.

Peter knew about her past. She never expected he would mention it again, especially at a time like this, when she was almost naked, offering what little worth she still had left.

"Don't you think I know that already?" Tara

stood and backed away from the bed. "I've always wished I could take it all back. Be braver or stronger. Wished that I'd told someone." She anchored her hand over her mouth and trapped in a sob. "I'll never be able to take it back." Shaking fingers twisted around her limp curls. "Never."

"Tara. I was just—"

"Trying to help?" She backed toward the door. Her heart shattered, opening a deep wound in a place she didn't know existed. A place that was tender and fragile. A tiny place left untainted with regret, now in ruins.

Watching him reach out to her, all she couldn't think of was how perfect he was. Flawless, gentle, and kind—a healer, an ability only given to someone with a pure, sincere heart. She was just a used up, worn out girl with nothing to offer him.

She squared her jaw, gathering the courage to do what she knew was right. The words scraped through her mind, up her throat, and finally out of her mouth in a shaky whisper. "No." She glanced at the box still in his hand. "No to getting married." She snatched her robe off the floor and slipped it on, then opened the door and lingered on the threshold. Unable to look him in the eyes, she stared into the empty hall as she forced the rest out of her lips. "No to us."

CHAPTER FIVE

Tara passed through crowds of people on the street, sobbing until her chest ached. A few people stared, but she didn't care. She just wiped her cheeks dry and waited for more to stream down her face.

A shiver wracked her body. Tara slipped her hands in her jacket pockets to draw the garment tighter around her. Tucked inside, her fingers brushed the plastic bag and small card.

Damn it. She'd forgotten to throw the pills away when that Malachi guy turned up. Thankfully Peter didn't find them or he would have thought she wasn't just going crazy, but on drugs too.

A black, low riding convertible sped past her and parked at a neighboring building drenched in neon lights under the bold letters on the vertical sign.

Club Grunge

She paused and pulled out the business card from her pocket. Two girls in designer dresses stepped out of the sports car. Long legs in short skirts, they could have had booming carriers as supermodels. One of them handed a valet the key. They strutted down the carpet in six-inch stilettos that matched their ruby lips. The two sauntered past security, straight into the club.

When the door swung open, Tara glimpsed colorful laser lights from inside. The heavy bass of a beat pounded into the street. Maybe a distraction would lift the layer of depression weighing on her—at least for now. Until she was reminded of the fact her relationship with Peter would never work out. Then it would start all over again.

As much as she wanted to believe they could be together, he was immortal and she was ordinary. It was doomed to fail.

Tara tore off her coat, exposing her bare shoulders and lacy tank top. It was what she chose on a whim before running out of the hotel. It was also one of the only outfits that fit her anymore since she'd dropped so much weight.

The fresh wound in her heart throbbed when she imagined Peter in his room, staring at the open box on his bedside table. If she had only seen it sooner, she could have spared them both.

She pushed away the thought and pressed forward.

Pacing toward the club, one obstacle stood between her and a night of mindless dancing. Security. The guard's broad shoulders looked as if they might split open his suit jacket if he inhaled too deeply. He clenched a clipboard between his thick fingers, scanning the line of patrons waiting to get in.

When she finally reached the front door, his less than impressed expression couldn't be a good sign. She'd have to talk her way in. She was, after all, the princess of persuasion in most other situations. She'd figure something out.

She gathered her hair over her shoulder and smiled. "Hi there."

His lips tightened. "Name."

Tara gestured to the line. "Let's be honest. Most of these people aren't on your list."

He dragged his gaze over her body, and as if giving his approval, extended his hand. "ID."

"Yeeahh." She smacked her lips. "About that."

He lowered his hand. "You're not on the list, and you don't have any ID, but you still want me to let you in?" He shooed her away. "Get lost."

"I have money." She extended some Russian currency. "It's enough, right?"

He examined the bills. "If you had an ID, I might make an exception about the list. Sorry." He waved a few of the people in line through the red velvet rope.

"Hey, Raco." A tall man with dark hair displayed a wide, charming smile.

The bouncer responded with a nod. "What up, Mr. Green? How you doin'?"

"Can't complain. It's busy tonight."

"Sure is."

The crowd pushed against the man, and he bumped shoulders with Tara. She stumbled and caught herself on a metal pole used to organize the line.

The man straightened his coat and turned to the

mob. "Hey, watch it!" He turned to Tara. "Sorry, Red. You all right?"

She nodded.

The bouncer looked at her. "I told you, lady. No ID, no entrance." He pointed to the street. "Now, please move away so I can let some of the other guests inside."

"What do you have in your hand?" The man took the business card from her and inspected it. He held it up, pinched between two fingers. "Where did you get this?"

She shrugged, not really in the mood to get into the whole story with a total stranger. He examined her for a moment, and then turned back to the bouncer. "She's not on the list?"

The bouncer shook his head.

Mr. Green thwacked the clipboard. "Sure she is." His finger lay over the paper. "She's listed as my guest."

The bouncer stared at the man. "Sir, she doesn't have an ID. She could be sixteen for all I know."

"What are you talking about?" The man straightened the bouncer's tie. "She just showed you her ID. I saw her."

The bouncer hesitated before lowering his clipboard. "Of course, Mr. Green. I must have missed it." He lifted the shiny hook from the pole, and pulled the velvet rope aside.

For whatever reason, the boss man wanted to let her in, and she wouldn't look a gift horse in the mouth. She followed him into the club while avoiding eye contact with the bouncer, who was clearly annoyed.

As she stepped through the door, strobe lights and the scent of sweat and cologne engulfed her.

Time to blow off some steam.

The rumble of the bass vibrated against her skin, followed by the flash of bright lights from an impressive laser show. A sea of dancers pulsed on the main floor, below a DJ who stood on an elevated stage overlooking several bars scattered around the lower level.

The guy who had let her in the club vanished into the crowd. She did the same—in the opposite direction. After shoving her way to a seat at a bar, she set some money on the counter. The pretty barista grabbed the cash and shoved it into a jar, already overflowing with bills. "What do you want?" she shouted over the music.

Tara raised her eyebrows. What *did* she want? She'd never ordered a drink before. "Just give me the cheapest drink you have."

The woman grabbed a bottle out of the fridge, popped the top off, and set it in front of her.

Tara slipped the bag out of her pocket and emptied the round pills into her palm. They looked so innocent. Pink and tiny, how much damage could they really do? With a disregard for rationality, she slipped them between her lips and swallowed them down with a swig of the bubbly drink.

She analyzed the taste, and then frowned. "Not such a big deal," she mumbled before setting the bottle back onto the bar top.

"So, what do you think?" The man in the expensive suit who'd let her in had returned, and now leaned against the stone bar.

She scratched a nervous itch on her arm. "About what?"

"My club."

She sat back in her chair. "*Your* club, huh?"

"That's right." He trailed his fingers down her hair. She cringed away. It didn't seem right to let someone besides Peter tug on her curls. Besides, if he thought she owed him anything because he got her in—

"So, listen. If you need anything, just tell the bartender you're with Mr. Green. That's my work name around these parts. What's your name?"

She shrugged. "I don't have one." More like she wasn't going to tell him.

"Really?" He stretched out the word and grinned. "A nameless beauty. Then I'll call you Red. We'll be a perfect pair." He took a step back. "Okay, Red. Have a good time. I'm sure I'll see you again." He set the business card on the bar top, and with a few steps, vanished back into the crowd.

She huffed. Red. What a stupid nickname. Still, it was better than him knowing her real name.

A strange, tingly sensation crawled up the back of her arms. Her vision blurred around the edges, and, all at once, her muscles sighed with relief.

Whatever that drug was, she hadn't been so relaxed in weeks. The glittery, marble bar top danced and twinkled through the liquid in her bottle. Flecks of light winked up through the air, and for her own personal entertainment, rose above her head like a tropical dance of fireflies. The twinkling lights, mixed with the lasers from the club's light show, were mesmerizing. Every cell inside her body prickled with energy rattling to escape. Her mind buzzed and suddenly, all she wanted to do was dance.

With her fingers wrapped around the neck of the glass bottle, she hopped off the barstool and maneuvered through the crowd. The floor shook with the fast tempo of the bass thumping through the speakers. Neon green lights flashed with the beat. Beams tickled the outstretched hands of the dancers.

Tara swigged more of her drink. The bubbles danced on her taste buds. Bobbing her head with the music, her body throbbed with elation. It was the first time since the horrifying memories flooded back that she could truly breathe.

She just wanted to *be*.

Be happy.

Be dancing.

Be away from everything that made her sad.

This was clearly the place to *be*.

Either her eyes were playing tricks on her, or the drugs had taken full effect. Ghostly figures of clubbers blurred over each other, creating a rippling sea of waves. The beat seemed to whisper words of endearment while she enjoyed the fluid movement of swaying her hips.

An explosion of laser lights burst around her, cued by another song. Excited screams from the crowd rushed adrenaline through Tara's body. She followed the crowd's lead, jumping up and down to a rhythm with her hands pumping in the air.

It must have been hours later when Tara's mind wandered back to reality. Breathless, she still clung onto her empty bottle. For how long, she wasn't sure. Drenched in sweat, she wove through the crowd to the exit. When she stepped outside, the night air smacked her face.

Even without her jacket, it was strange she wasn't in the least bit cold.

White clouds puffed from her lips without a goose bump in sight. In fact, she still felt pretty damn good.

The twinkling stars in the sky carried a feeling of nostalgia. She missed Renato's house in Belize. The evenings there were just as clear, but with the sound of crashing ocean waves and salt in the air. Back there, life was easier.

She checked the time on her cell phone. Four o'clock in the morning. Two missed calls from Peter. He must have been worried. He had every right to be. She'd slapped him down and then took off. Damn it. She had to talk to him and make him understand. He deserved better.

She could see it all laid out in front of her. Her mind had become so clear. Everything she had done to him…to herself. She was a giant smudge on his otherwise perfect existence, and he was the only guy who had ever really loved her.

She typed a text to Peter.

Tara: I'm okay. Coming back. We need to talk.

She flipped her phone shut and drew in a deep breath. Energy pulsed through her veins. She could jog all the way back to the hotel if she wanted. Maybe across the city. What were those pills made of, anyway?

The same women who'd arrived in the sports car earlier that night were being escorted out of the club by Mr. Green. A lady on each arm, he signaled the valet to retrieve their car and dutifully waited until the girls pulled out of the parking lot.

When Mr. Green spotted her, he straightened his jacket. "Well, hello, Red. Calling it a night already?"

Two men exited the club and loitered behind him.

She smiled. In a much better mood than when they first met, it was only appropriate to be nice. "Yeah, I'm going to head back to my hotel."

He walked toward her, the cufflinks of his suit gleaming in the neon lights. "Be careful. Moscow's a dangerous place at night."

She couldn't help but notice his thin but handsome face and charming swag appeal. "You're not from around here, are you?"

"Is it that obvious?" He chuckled. "I'm American. Moved here about five years ago when a business opportunity arose."

"Oh, right." She gestured to the building. "Your club."

"My club is what I do for fun. What I do for work…well." He slid his hands in his pants pockets. "I think you've already had the pleasure of sampling some of my *merchandise*."

Tara muffled a gasp. How the hell did he know about that? One thing was for sure. She'd play dumb. Very dumb.

"Andrei doesn't give out free samples often," he

continued. "So when I saw that particular business card, I knew you were a special guest. I called him and he told me about the sad redhead at the restaurant." He rocked back and forth from his heels to the balls of his feet. His gaze moved over her shoulder, and his pleasant smile vanished.

Tara glanced behind her.

Malachi stood on the sidewalk, his gaze locked on her. "What did I tell you about these people?" He walked toward her with no hint of emotion in his tone.

"Malachi." Mr. Green's lip curled. "How ya feeling, friend? I heard—"

"You heard wrong." Malachi stopped beside Tara.

Her gaze darted between them. "I'm guessing you know each other?"

Malachi gave Mr. Green an up and down glance. "You could say that." Malachi's cold fingers wrapped around her arm. "I suggest you stop associating with the town garbage," he mumbled, too low for Mr. Green to hear.

A rock formed in Tara's stomach, and for the first time since she left the club, the cold wound around her spine. "Uh…" She stared down at his fingers, white as snow with black polished nails. "Maybe I should just go."

Mr. Green straightened his suit and stood in silence while Malachi dragged her down the street, his grip on her arm like iron. The effects of the drugs were beginning to wear off, and she struggled to keep up with his pace.

"You just can't seem to keep yourself out of

trouble, can you?"

"Uh…" She had to work for every breath. "Slow down." The rubber soles of her shoes skidded across the sidewalk until she came to a stop and slumped against a brick building. She rubbed her chest. "Damn it. My chest hurts."

"Well what did you expect? I told you not to—" Malachi's eyes widened. He grabbed her arm again. "Come here." He pulled her into a dark, narrow alley and shoved her back against a wall.

The echo of shoes slapping against concrete pounded in her ears. "Where'd they go?" A man's voice said from the street.

"They came this way."

The distant shape of two men lingered on the sidewalk. "What do they want?" Her voice echoed off the narrow-set walls, carrying farther than she expected, and catching the men's attention.

The men stalked toward them. "Well, well. It's true. Malachi's back." The tall guy's lanky arms swayed at his sides while he strutted like a rooster. "You're one tough son of a bitch."

Malachi stepped into the middle of the alley.

Still leaning against the wall, Tara recognized the men who had flanked Mr. Green outside the club.

Searing pain shot through her head, and the images of the men blurred. "What do they want?" Tara said again.

"They want you," Malachi responded quietly.

She sure as hell didn't have any intention of going with them. One step at a time, she inched down the wall. Her hands dragged over the seams of the bricks while she strained to peer deeper into the dark alley.

Malachi glanced back at her. "I suggest you stay close unless you want to be taken."

She stopped and stared at him in horror. "Taken?"

"Mr. Green doesn't much like it when a client runs out on him." The tall, skinny man with a rat face pointed at her. Brass knuckles gleamed on his clenched fist.

Malachi squared his stance. "She's not an offering."

The second man—a muscular Russian with a jagged scar across his cheek—stepped forward. "What belongs to our boss, belongs to us."

Tara held her breath in an effort not to pant like a fat dog in mid-summer, but she couldn't help it. She'd gone from shivering from the night's cold, to heat exploding throughout every cell of her body. Even without a jacket, the urge to strip to cool down overwhelmed her. A bead of sweat rolled down the curve of her neck and between her breasts. She rubbed her face. "What's happening to me?"

"Mr. Green says she's an offering," said the tall one. "Now move aside so we can collect." Malachi stepped into the light of an old street lamp. The yellow tinted glow revealed his face from the shroud of darkness. The thug stepped back. "Damn, man. What's wrong with your eyes?"

The Russian gave a low laugh. "Halloween is over." He waved a thick blade in front of Malachi's face while displaying his grill of gold teeth. "Or maybe you need a broken nose to go with your black eyes." He dragged the pointed metal tip down Malachi's chest.

Malachi stood perfectly still as the blade tapped along the buttons of his jacket. Malachi grabbed the thug's wrist and aimed the knife at his heart. "Go ahead," he growled. "Do it."

"You must be crazier than we thought."

Malachi puffed his chest, tempting the tip to drive deeper. "I guess we can find out."

"Stop fucking around," the tall guy said. "Just kill him and let's get the girl." He pulled out a burlap sack from his jacket and glanced over his shoulder. "Mr. Green wants her back before she crashes. Hurry up before he comes down here himself. Then he'll really be pissed."

Malachi clicked with his tongue. "I wouldn't do that."

A full-blown laugh bellowed from the Russian's gut. "What are you going to do about it?"

Malachi tilted his head. "Let's find out, unless you're too much of a coward."

The Russian scowled. He gripped Malachi's shoulder, and with a swift thrust, drove the knife deep into Malachi's chest.

Tara gasped and suppressed the urge to vomit. Panic thrashed through her, pulling out a scream, which echoed through the empty streets of Moscow.

Malachi stumbled back, staring down at the blade protruding from his chest. Blood dribbled from the corner of his mouth, and he fell to his knees, fingers curled around the weapon's handle.

The shadow of a man appeared in the alley's entrance. It lingered a moment, then disappeared in the direction of the club.

"Grab the girl and let's get the hell outta here," the tall thug said. "Shit. We have to make her stop screaming!"

The Russian grabbed Tara by the hair and pulled her to her feet. "Shut. Up."

She instantly quieted, too terrified to disobey.

They slipped the sack over her head and tightened it around her neck. Tara thrashed, peering through tiny gaps in the woven fibers. But she could only see shadows and not much else. The thug tied her arms behind her back and shoved her forward, but her legs gave out and she slapped to the pavement.

"Damn girls," said the taller man in his nasally tone. "I hate being the fucking collector."

"Move out of the way." Strong hands gripped her and threw her over a shoulder, knocking the wind out of her lungs. Claustrophobia suffocated her every breath. The Russian huffed. "Let's go."

Unconsciousness tempted her mind, pulling her in and out of awareness. The sweet, metallic scent of blood filled the darkness—Malachi's blood. God. They'd killed him and just left him there on the dirty ground. She held her breath, too afraid to cry.

The Russian spun around. Tara's stomach churned from the sudden whirl. "Where is he?" the Russian bellowed.

"What the…he was right there."

"I killed him."

A whisper caressed Tara's ear. "Who? Me?"

The Russian dropped Tara to the ground. Her head smacked against the concrete, making her ears ring.

"What the fuck is that!"

A horrific scream gave Tara the motivation to push to her knees. She shook her head, trying to lose the sack, but it wouldn't budge.

"Get away from me!" the tall man shouted. "No! No!"

She huddled against the wall and pressed her body as close to the cold brick as possible. When the stink of rotting flesh shot up her nose, she curled into a ball and pressed her face to her knees in a futile attempt to block the noxious reek. Instead, the putrid smell coated her tongue.

Someone grasped her arm and pulled her up. She screamed and stumbled forward before falling to her knees. The skin under her jeans burned with road rash.

"Calm down."

She gasped and froze, sure she was disoriented. She couldn't have heard what she thought—Malachi's voice. Yet it somehow brought a strange sense of relief.

Her eyes wide, she strained to peer through the gaps in the sack. "Take this thing off my head!"

He worked the tie loose and yanked it off. She stared into his face—the face of a man who should have been dead. She'd seen the Russian stab him. She'd watched Malachi fall to the ground.

His eyes were nearly normal now, the dark circles almost completely gone. His clothes were stained with blood, but the knife wasn't in his chest anymore and he was alive. Not just alive, but seemingly unharmed. How could he possibly be?

She glanced down the alley.

"Don't look. You don't want to see what's over there." He scooped her into his arms. "Relax, I have you. You're about to crash."

CHAPTER SIX

The roots crawled around her legs, shooting pain through her body with each tightening coil. Unable to kick them away, and with her hands tied behind her back, she was left helpless to watch them slither toward the wounds on her legs.

"Get away from me!" Massive red thorns extended from the vines and dug into her skin. They snaked up her limbs, and a woody tip brushed against the open wounds on her knees. Tara tried to rock to the side and flip the chair; she'd forgotten it was not an ordinary seat. Her efforts only exhausted what little energy she had left. She whimpered, and slumped forward in defeat.

Delicate membranes clustered beneath the transparent bark and throbbed with thirst. Each capillary morphed into a deeper red as it invaded her body.

Tara's screams bounced off the stone walls, cueing the other inmates in neighboring cells to sob and wail.

Barbed vines pushed deeper, elevating her skin as they slithered around bone and muscle.

Her screaming was cut off by the nightmarish awareness of roots working up the inside of her thigh, and moments later, around her ribs.

***

Light shined through the windows, waking Tara in a cold sweat. She had almost gotten used to peeling damp hair from her forehead and neck every time she awoke.

Thankfully, the gold and burgundy drapes of Peter's room marked a sanctuary, and her muscles relaxed into the down feather comforter.

Peter's room had become her favorite, no matter where in the world they were. Not the room itself, but his energy in it. It blanketed the space with tranquility.

Her inner peace vanished when her mind snapped back to the last time they'd spoken. She'd broken his heart—and hers. He probably thought she didn't want him, which was the furthest from the truth.

A man cleared his throat. Tara startled and sat up to see Renato, sitting on a fabric chaise on the opposite side of the room, his ankle crossed over his knee and a pipe in his mouth.

Tara gripped the blanket and pulled it over her chest. She still had on her tank top and jeans, but for some reason felt indecent.

"Good morning." Renato's tone seemed calmer than normal. He examined her with a placid stare. "Tara, why did you keep your struggles from us?"

She swallowed. "I guess Peter told you."

"He did, though he waited much too long."

She hung her head. "It's not his fault. I didn't want him to."

Renato sat silent for a moment, puffing his pipe. His gaze was lost to the view of Moscow through the arched window, seemingly contemplating his next words. "Tara, do you not trust me?"

"It's not that I don't trust you. It's just that…I didn't want to be the crazy girl again. I spent my whole life with doctors telling me I have PTSD, and that my self-confidence was stripped away by…well, my past. Someone was always trying to fix me." She dropped her gaze. "I just wanted to keep my clean slate, I guess."

"And Peter? Do you have any idea what kind of stress you put him under, asking him to withhold that kind of information?"

"Peter," she whispered, the fresh wound in her heart tearing open again. "Where is he?"

"In the lobby. I asked him to allow us to speak privately."

She exhaled, hoping some of the heartache would lessen with it. No such luck. "As long as he's okay—"

"I did not in any way imply that he is okay." Renato uncrossed his legs and placed both of his feet firmly on the floor. He leaned forward. "What you did to assist us in finding Sarian was a brave act." He slowly rested his back against the chaise again, his fingers gliding absentmindedly over the etchings of his bone pipe. "But refusing to inform us of your deterioration has come at a price. I spoke with Marzena and there is nothing she can do to lock your memories away now. There is nothing anyone can do."

"So…" She bit her lip. "I'm stuck with them?"

"Unfortunately, yes. But now—" He stood and walked toward her, stopping at the foot of her bed. "Now we are faced with yet another puzzle. Who is the boy?"

Flashes of a dark alley, the gleam of a blade, and the metallic smell of blood darted through her mind. "Malachi."

"How do you know him?"

"I don't. I mean, not really." She'd nearly forgotten about the entire incident. "Is he here?"

"No. But he did press the panic button on your cell phone. Peter and I tracked the satellite signal to a bus stop, nearly three miles away."

She twisted the blankets in her hands, hoping Renato hadn't noticed her cheeks flush with heat. It served her right. She didn't have anyone to blame but herself.

"Malachi was following me around. Then Mr. Green and those guys…" She could still hear the Russian's blood curdling screams.

There was a knock on the door. Renato's features tensed. "I believe that's Peter." He gave a chastising stare. "It would be humane of you to offer him some explanations. I have never seen him so torn."

His words cut through any ounce of self-pity she had. As if a lead weight had been slammed against her chest, she could barely breathe. Renato was right. She'd crushed Peter and given him every reason to hate her.

Renato opened the door and silently left the

room, passing Peter in the hall. Peter lingered in the doorway, his hands shoved in his pockets and his head hung low. Tara's heart nearly collapsed with guilt.

He ground the toe of his sneaker on the carpet in silence.

"I…" She wasn't sure exactly what to say. But whatever it was, she didn't want to shout it across the room. "Can you come closer?"

He hesitated before dragging himself to the center of the room, several feet from her bed. His eyes were hidden under layers of shaggy brown hair.

"Peter…" She would have to talk to him while he treated her like the plague, not that she deserved better. "I don't know what to say—"

"Is he why you said no?" His voice was quiet, but clearly streaked with pain. He met her gaze for the first time. "Is he why you don't want me?"

"God, Peter, no. I swear to you, I have *never*…" She pushed to her knees while on the mattress and planted her hands on his chest. His heart raced under her fingers.

Every cell in her body urged her to grovel and beg for forgiveness, but she couldn't give in. He deserved to be with someone who wouldn't break his heart. She had to do the right thing, even if it tore her apart. And after, she would spend the rest of her life in regret. Regret that she would forever miss the scent of fresh rain when they kissed. Regret that his gentle touch would someday fall over someone else's cheek.

No matter how much she desired to be with him,

there was one thing that would never change.

He was eternal, and she would never be anything more than an ordinary girl.

Nothing special about her.

Not immortal.

And certainly not good enough.

Tara bit her lip. "What do you want me to say? That I love you?" She shook her head. "I've never loved anyone so much." Tears welled in her eyes. "And I don't think I'll ever love anyone like this again."

"But you said—"

"What I said…" Her muscles screamed to wrap her arms around him and hold him close. "You deserve better, Peter. Someone not…used. Someone who will never leave you." She hung her head. "I can never be the girl you really need. I'll always be damaged, and worse, just human. Someday I'll die and you'll be left alone. That's not what you want for yourself, really. You just don't know it yet."

"What the hell are you talking about?" He hooked his finger under her chin and tilted her face up. "What do you mean, used?"

His hand slid from her face when she lowered back down to the mattress. "Peter…" She pulled her knees to her chest. "I'm not the shiny new penny you want. I've been…" Her skin crawled. "Spent."

"Damn you, Tara." He grabbed her shoulders firmly and pulled her off the bed to her feet. "If I hear you say anything like that again, I swear…" His furious gaze was hazed with desperation. "I love you, no matter what happened before, and whether you're human or not. That doesn't matter.

You're not used or broken or damaged, and as long as you're alive, I want to be with you." As he searched her face, his eyes softened. "You're an angel."

She pursed her lips, trapping in a sob.

He cradled her against his chest.

Her heart mourned for her innocence robbed, for the years spent feeling dirty and ashamed, and most of all, it mourned for what she was about to do.

Even if Peter did accept her, it would be impossible to escape time.

She gently drew away from him. "What if we *did* get married? What would our kids be like? Have you ever thought about that? Would they be like you, or me? Maybe one would be Riyata, and the other would be ordinary. You'll have to not only bury me, but our child. Is that what you really want?"

"Kids?" A soft smile played over his lips. "I didn't know you thought about that already."

"This isn't a joke, Peter." Her tone became sharp. "You don't realize what you're asking for. You don't see that marrying me would screw up your entire life."

Peter's grin vanished. "So you don't want to be with me anymore? Just like that?"

"It's not about what I want. It's about what's right." She had to be strong. The more upset she appeared, the harder this would be for him. If she could just mask her grief for a few moments, she could force herself to walk out the door and do him the biggest favor of his life. "The point is, if you really love someone, you want what's best for them, not what's best for yourself. And what's best for you is to be with someone who won't leave you. If we end this now—" The words nearly scalded her tongue, but she forced them out. "It'll give you time to get over us, and move—" She gripped her stomach that cramped with protest, and drew in a deep breath. "You can move on."

Peter shook his head. "You don't mean that." He took a step back, his finger jabbing the air. "I know you love me, Tara. I know you do, and you can't do this!" His hand dropped to his side. He whispered, "Please, don't do this."

She put more space between them as she walked toward the door. "One day you'll see that I'm doing you a favor. I know it doesn't seem like it now, but one day, you'll look back and thank me."

***

The next day, Tara walked through the sunny streets of Moscow, watching the locals browse the produce market in the food district. The first time she visited this area, she and Peter were searching for Contessa. The temptress lived just a block away, but if Tara never saw that woman again, it would be too soon.

Mounds of colorful fruits were piled on wooden carts. Market workers weighed, priced, and handed over the merchandise before waving goodbye.

If only she could be one of those people. Anyone. A young woman with a scarf covering her hair hovered her nose over a peach. A warm smile cast over her lips while she counted several into a bag. She would be fine. The woman looked so peaceful. Why couldn't Tara simply snap her fingers and be the woman with the scarf? Have a completely different life.

She sighed.

The bitter smell of cigarettes pulled her out of her daydream. Tara coughed and waved her hand in front of her face, fully aware who was nearby. "You know that habit will kill you."

Malachi grinned. "I highly doubt that."

She narrowed her eyes. "You really have to stop appearing out of nowhere. You're like a freaking phantom."

His winked. "I'll take that as a compliment." He flicked the ash from his cigarette and took another drag. "So, are you better today?"

"I guess I owe you a thank you, don't I?"

He shrugged.

"Well…" Another nervous itch ate at her arm. She scratched it, and glanced at him. "Thanks."

He silently watched the crowds of people, inhaling another drag.

It was time to get to the bottom of this. "Who are you, Malachi? Really."

"In what way are you asking?"

"Is there more than one?"

"Yes."

She examined the lack of black under his eyes. "You toned down the makeup today."

He flicked more ashes from his cigarette. "It's not makeup."

"Really? So all the black around your eyes is…" She shrugged one shoulder and waited for him to respond.

"A curse."

"A curse," she said, more as a statement than a question. He stepped forward, his gaze locked with hers. In the light of midday, the black shadows were hardly noticeable. But when she looked more closely, it didn't seem like makeup at all. The darkness was buried deep in his skin. Tara backed away. Maybe she should hear him out. "What kind of curse?"

Malachi gestured to the fruits stacked on the stands. "Did you come here to buy something?"

"Not really." She examined at the peaches, and then gripped her stomach. "I'm not hungry." The truth was she'd give anything to be able to eat one of the fruits. Just a bite.

He nodded. "Yeah, me either. Not anymore."

There was something really, really wrong with this guy. What he did to protect her the night before was certainly not normal. But she still had no idea why Mr. Green's men had gone after her. If she wanted to find out, she'd have to stick around. "What did those guys want?"

"Let's walk." Malachi paced down the sidewalk. Tara followed, jogging to catch up before she fell into stride.

He hooked his thumbs in the front pockets of his pants and cast his gaze to the cobblestone walkway. "That drug Andrei gave you is called Drop5. It's new, from some dealer in Japan."

"And how do you know Mr. Green?"

"I used to work for him. The drug is supposed to make the collection of offerings easier."

Her chest tightened. "What do you mean, offerings?"

He glanced around as if watching out for anyone listening. "Those guys don't just traffic drugs," he said in a hushed voice. "It took me a while to find you. You're here with the guardian, right?"

Tara furrowed her brow. "What do you want with Zanya?"

He suddenly spoke with more urgency. "Not me, but something is happening that she's not aware of, and if we don't stop it, Sarian will have all the power he needs to not only control the book, but to overthrow the underworld. Next is the middleworld. Nobody will be able to stop him. Not even your little team."

"How do you know about all of this? I thought only Riyata knew about Sarian and the underworld." Her lips parted. "Wait. Are *you* Riyata?"

"Unfortunately, no." The lines in his mouth deepened with a frown. "Maybe if I were, I could have done something."

"About what?"

He rubbed the back of his neck. "Nothing. Never mind. The point is, Sarian is working hard to get enough power to make sure nobody is able to take the throne from him once he has it. But he wants something else. The more human sacrifices that are made in his name, the more power he'll have to take whatever he wants—including your friend."

"I don't get how all of this works together. Why is he using drugs?"

They turned a corner and continued into the

shopping district of the city. Fruit carts and the scent of earthy spices were replaced with windows of boutiques selling clothes and purses.

"Sarian doesn't care how he gets what he wants, and even though the king of the underworld would tear him apart if he knew, Sarian has resorted to using humans to do his dirty work. He's promised to give them certain powers once he is strong enough to overthrow the underworld king." He huffed. "Better to be on the right hand of Satan than in his way, right?" He raked his fingers through his hair. "Anyway. The drug is used to make it easier to handle the girls until it's their time. Meanwhile, the guys have their fun with the girls."

Tara's stomach rolled. "What?"

"Nothing's off limits. The girls are just toys for them until—" He glanced at her. "After five hours of high, it makes you crash, and unless you're lucky enough to have someone around to protect you, they collect. Mr. Green is the one in charge of this district, but he's not the highest ranking."

"So if you weren't there that night…"

"You'd be gone."

She rubbed her face, her skin clammy and cold to the touch. With Zanya still on her rescue mission, and she and Peter on the rocks, she would have to go to Renato for help. Until Zanya returned, Renato would know what to do. They would figure it out together. "I need to get back to the hotel."

He stopped and planted his palms on either side of her against a building, caging her in place. Tara pressed her hands against his chest to keep him at a distance.

"You can't leave. We have unfinished business."

Her body heat spiked and her muscles tensed. "What is that supposed to mean?"

He slowly dropped his hands to his sides. "You owe me a favor, and payoff starts *now*."

CHAPTER SEVEN

With clothes shoved into her backpack, Tara zipped it closed and took one last look at the empty hotel room.

Malachi's story weighed heavy on her. How anyone could do such things to those girls was unbearable to consider.

Malachi needed to get back in with Mr. Green's gang, work his way up the badass ladder, and get to the boss, who was working beside Sarian. Apparently, the man was pretty elusive. Since Malachi had never actually met him before, it made their plan much more difficult.

Tara's heart was constantly pulled back to the thought of those girls—torn away from their families and friends to be thrown into this mess. She slumped against the bedpost. Her muscles throbbed. The dizzy spells had gotten worse. She closed her eyes and drew in a deep breath, her fingers tightening around the wood pole.

If she decided to do this—if she agreed to be Malachi's bait in order to find the boss, and delay Sarian's plan long enough for Zanya and the others to stop him once and for all—she'd have to be sure.

Sure she wouldn't want to turn back.

Sure she would be willing to take the risk.

Sure that if something went terribly wrong, she'd still think it was worth it, as long as they caught the bastard in charge.

Her stomach twisted. Plotting a murder had never been on her bucket list, but she wouldn't be the one to kill him. Her job was to help Malachi find him, and he'd take it from there. That was the deal. Besides, filth like the boss-man didn't belong in the human gene pool, and she wouldn't feel bad over him being wiped from the face of the earth. She knew exactly what those girls would deal with if they survived. None of her mom's boyfriends were ever caught, and she was still paying the price.

She had to get out of her hotel room before someone came looking for her. With a sweater layered over her clothes, she pulled her curls into a messy bun, and then typed a text to Peter. If she was going to leave, he deserved a goodbye, no matter how short or vague.

Tara: I'm leaving for a while. Be back when Zanya gets home. Need some space.

She couldn't tell him the truth. He would never understand why she needed to do this. She pressed send and took one last look at her hotel room. Both beds were perfectly made. She hadn't slept in her room since her encounter with Mr. Green, and Zanya's bed hadn't been touched since she left.

She stared silently at where her best friend had

last slept. Zanya still hadn't called. All Tara could do was hope for the best and try to survive the next few days without the protection of Renato and Peter.

She wrapped her fingers around the straps of her backpack, inspecting herself in the full-length mirror mounted on the wall.

Life had changed so much in the last six months. She didn't even recognize herself. Her gaze moved down to the clothes hanging over her body, with her belt tightened yet another notch.

"Tara?" Peter called from the hall before he knocked.

Her gaze flew to the door. Damn it. She should have waited to send the text until after she left.

"Tara." He knocked again. "Are you in there?"

She bit her lip. His voice was so warm and familiar. She wanted more than anything to let him in, but if she did, things would get messy.

The green light on the door lock lit up and he pushed it ajar.

Tara slipped onto the balcony as quietly as she could. With her back pressed against the building, hidden behind a patio palm in a terracotta pot, she listened to Peter's footsteps drag over the carpet. "Tara?" The door to the bathroom creaked open, followed by silence.

Tara tightened her grip around the guardrail as she listened to the plush down comforter exhaled under his weight when he sat on her bed. How did things come to this—her hiding from the guy she'd do anything for?

The footsteps returned and grew louder. She

glanced at the balcony doors she'd left ajar and squeezed her eyes shut, silently cursing herself for not covering her trail.

He gently slid open the doors. The toes of his shoes appeared, barely visible over the threshold. She couldn't see his face. Thank God for that. If she did, her self-discipline would likely cave. She had to show some restraint, for his sake. Anchoring her feet to the floor, she clamped her lips shut. A gust of cold wind swept a tear off her cheek.

Peter exhaled and moved back into the room. Moments later, was gone.

***

Her backpack was all that accompanied her on the restaurant patio while sitting across the street from the dark sedan. She watched Andrei tap his fingers on the leather steering wheel. More quickly than she anticipated, her efforts to catch his attention paid off.

Andrei stepped out of his car and crossed the street. Within moments, he pulled out the chair across from her. His muscular arms were perfectly matched by his baritone voice. "May I sit?"

She nodded.

He sat and laced his fingers on top o the table, tapping his thumbs together. "So, you are back to see me."

She didn't reply. There was no doubt he had heard of her encounter with Mr. Green's thugs and that they'd failed to collect her that night. Any slip up could blow her cover.

He leaned forward, his eyes narrow. "You are not alone in Moscow."

She was there to play a part, but his statement evoked more emotion than she anticipated. It was the opposite from the truth. "I am alone," she whimpered. "Me and my boyfriend just broke up and my best friend is gone, doing God knows what—" She cradled her head in her hands. "And to top it all off, there's some weird guy following me, and I got jumped in an alley after I went to that Club Grunge place in town." She sniffled, and mumbled, "I guess I have bad luck no matter where I'm at." The sorrow stirring deep inside her was raw and harsh. "I'm leaving." She kicked at her backpack.

He raised a bushy eyebrow. "Really?"

"I can't stand being here anymore."

He leaned back in his chair. "Where will you go, my dear?" Suddenly his tone became soft and laden with concern. Clearly she wasn't the only one who could put on a good show.

She shrugged. "I don't know. Don't care. Just out of Moscow."

"But Moscow can be a very fun place, if you know the right people." He ran his fingers down his goatee. "Did you enjoy the taste?"

She sighed. "I lost it."

"What a shame. That was very expensive."

"Yeah. Sorry. It wasn't my fault, though. I put it in my jacket pocket, and someone stole my coat." She shivered, wearing a thin sweater that was zipped up as far as it would go; not much of a shield from the cold. She sat a moment longer before grabbing her backpack off the ground. "Well, I better get going. I need to catch the next bus out of here."

He reached across the table. The mere presence of his hand in front of her caused her to freeze. "Before you go, maybe you would come to a party. I think I have one more sample for you."

Tara paused, as if considering her options. She didn't want to be too obvious and give away the fact this was exactly what she wanted—an invitation into the club, or any other place that would end in her being taken. But not by him. Not now. She needed Malachi to protect her when it all went down, and, for the moment, he was nowhere in sight.

Tara shrugged. "I'll think about it."

He smiled and stood. "Good. I will see you tomorrow night. Come to the club. I will be looking for you." As soon as Andrei returned to his car, Tara grabbed her bag and quietly left the restaurant.

***

She waited at the glass-paneled bus stop, perusing the bus schedule to kill time. There were no more stops for the night, and Malachi had exactly two minutes to show up before he was officially late.

Footsteps crunched over a thin layer of freshly fallen snow until he emerged from the darkness. As usual, he'd dressed in all black. Except this time he was suave in a button down dress shirt and a pair of black slacks, wearing a silver watch instead of rows of leather bracelets. He looked almost normal. Malachi ran his fingers through his thick, black hair as he approached. He was handsome, in a grungy sort of way.

She sniffled, her nose runny from the cold. The gloves barely kept the bite off her fingers, and she'd be lucky not to get the flu without something heavier on than a sweater. She inspected Malachi's suit, incomplete without a jacket. "You must be freezing."

"I'm fine." He gestured with a nod of his head. "Let's go."

She followed him down the street to an old, abandoned building marked with graffiti. Tara tiptoed around shards of shattered glass scattered over the sidewalk while Malachi worked open the lock with a tool.

"What is this place?"

"I'm staying here for now."

"Here?" She glanced around the dark and quiet neighborhood.

There was a click, and the lock popped. He pushed the front door open and held it for her. "Come on in."

Tara's teeth chattered. "I swear, if you end up being some kind of psycho—"

His eyebrow arched. "You'll what?"

He was right. There would be nothing she could do if he turned out not to be who he said he was— not that he'd explained who he really was to begin with. But she needed to do this. She needed to help him, help those girls, and help herself. She huffed and stepped inside. "Fine."

Three flights of stairs later, they entered what used to be a corner office with tiled floors, and rows of fluorescent lights that probably hadn't been turned on for years. One wall was floor to ceiling windows, showcasing a vast view of Moscow. Tara gazed out at the city lights twinkling in the distance.

Malachi shut the door. "So what happened?"

"He invited me to the club tomorrow night."

"There will be backup there. He doesn't want you to get away this time."

Her shoulders tensed. "I guess that makes sense."

Malachi crouched beside a mattress lying on the floor and rummaged through a duffle bag.

Tara noticed the stained ceiling tiles, some of them sagging and split. "How long have you been staying here?"

The cold radiated through the tile floors and windows. It reminded her of the orphanage in the winter. A chill crawled up her back.

"Catch." He tossed her a heavy sweater. "You'll wake up sick if you don't get something warm on."

She held out the garment while she swayed from side to side. Was it her, or had the room started spinning? The cold wasn't helping her body cope. She'd used up more energy trying to stay warm as shivers quaked her muscles.

Malachi slowly stood while examining her. "Are you okay?"

She slipped on the sweater and nodded.

Hell no, she wasn't okay.

She squinted, and accidentally rocked back on her heels, flailing her arms to stay balanced. Malachi grabbed her. It wasn't the gentlest embrace, but it grounded her.

"Thanks."

"What was that all about?"

"I just…" She rubbed her face. Her fingers were ice cold to the touch. "I haven't been sleeping great, that's all."

His eyes narrowed. "That's not all that's going on."

She yanked her arm out of his grip. "It's all you need to know," she mumbled. He squared his stance while she tried her best not to feel bad over her pissy tone.

There was an emotion in his eyes she recognized—regret, or maybe shame. She couldn't put her finger on it, but something was eating him from the inside out. "Why do you want to get back inside so bad?"

He didn't answer right away, but eventually caved. "They took someone I care about." His jaw tightened. "Those bastards need to get what's coming to them, and I'm just the guy to do it. But I can't do it alone, so…" He leaned against the wall. "Thanks for helping."

She hugged herself, savoring the slow-growing warmth from the extra layer. "I didn't think I had much of a choice."

He grinned. "No, you didn't. But still…"

Tara turned back to the sea of lights and watched as tiny cars drove over the winding roads, past illuminated signs, and through the shining city. "It's funny where life takes you." For some reason, she knew he'd understand. "My life went from miserable, to worse, to free, and now…" What she said next came out in a whisper. "I'm just *lost*."

"Is that why you agreed to help me? Because you have nowhere to go?"

His words carried so much truth—more than she could consider at the moment. "I guess," she said in a low voice. "Among other things. Plus you need to follow me through the process to get to the boss, and if taking him down will stop what he's doing to those women, I'm in."

She watched his reflection in the glass. He cocked his head to the side. "What *other things*?"

"Nothing I feel like talking about." She hung her head. "But I'm not useless. Even if I don't have superpowers, I know I can do something to change the world. Something that's worth remembering."

Malachi chuckled. "You wish you had superpowers, huh?"

"Whatever you want to call it." She glanced back at him. "You're not exactly normal. At least you can do something to stop what's going on. I wish I had that ability."

His features sobered. "Be careful what you wish for."

She rested her hand on the frosty window. The beautiful stars of frost melted under her touch. "If someone had been there," she said quietly, "if I could have done something, they wouldn't have hurt me." She dropped her hand to her side, leaving a foggy imprint on the glass. She cleared her throat and glanced at Malachi. "I mean, you know. In general."

"Right. In general." He dragged his bag off the mattress. "You take the bed."

CHAPTER EIGHT

The next evening, Tara pulled her curls into a messy bun and turned to Malachi. "You ready?"

He tucked a gun into the back of his pants and nodded.

She stared at the weapon. "Why are you bringing that?"

"Backup."

Tara arched a brow. "You didn't need any backup when Mr. Green's guy stuck a knife in your chest." Her question made him shift his weight. He still hadn't offered an explanation for that incident, but he would probably shut down if she pushed too hard. At any hint of curiosity about his real identity, he clammed up or danced around the subject.

He crossed the room and opened the door. "Let's go. I'll fill you in on some things while we walk."

Out of the building and onto the street, the thin layer of snow had melted from the sidewalk. A relief, considering all she had on was a lacy tank top and a pair of jeans that used to be tight on her, but were now borderline baggy. It would have to do. The more appealing she made herself look, the better. The baggy sweater Malachi had lent her the night before didn't do anything for her figure.

"Now listen," Malachi said quietly, walking in stride with her toward the club. "These guys are no joke. Mr. Green is working hard to get in Sarian's good favor, and he and his thugs will do just about anything to make that happen. But the system works like trafficking, and you should know what to expect when they take you. There are five stages to the process."

"Wait. Are these stages going to make me want to back out?"

"Maybe. But you need to know so you don't freak out when it's happening. You have to stay composed. When the time comes, you need to have a level head."

"And you used to actually work for these guys?"

"Not really. Well, kinda." He rubbed the back of his neck. "Where was I?"

She rolled her eyes. "Stages."

"Right. Five of them." He counted them out on his fingers as he spoke. "Collection, transportation, harboring, preparation and, well, you know how it ends."

"I have to ask. How are they targeting the girls? And why just girls?"

"A woman's blood is more valuable than a man's, and it depends on their age. The younger, the better. The sacrifice of a child has more power than an adult."

Tara's throat tightened. "A child?" She rested her hand on her chest.

"Don't think about that right now." They turned

a corner on the sidewalk. "Just keep it together. Follow through with the plan, and everything will be fine. We need a code phrase. Something that won't be too conspicuous, just in case we have to cut and run."

Tara nodded. "That's smart. Like what?"

He examined her for a moment.

Tara's cheeks flushed with heat, and she didn't know quite where to look. "What?"

"Your hair."

"What about it?"

"We'll use your hair for our code phrase. Just give me a minute to think."

It only took another few minutes to get to the street where the club was located. She and Malachi had just finished talking about the fine details—who not to screw with, to stay submissive, always keep her eyes and ears open—amongst other things. Soon the club was in sight. Malachi slipped his hand around Tara's waist. "They're going to be suspicious," he said. "Just remember everything we talked about. Act like you're here for a party. Play dumb."

"Wouldn't that be every man's dream?" He shot her a glare. She sighed. "Fine. Brainless ditz it is."

The same bouncer manned the door. His gaze locked on Malachi while they strutted toward the entrance. The bouncer's lips parted, and he fumbled with his clipboard.

"Hey, Raco," Malachi said in a pompous tone. "Long time no see." His confidence gave Tara a sense of reassurance—perhaps false, but she'd take what she could get. The large, dark-skinned bouncer clenched his jaw. "I think Mr. Green will be happy to see me." He pulled Tara closer. "Especially since I brought a guest."

The bouncer stared at Tara. Her belly fluttered, and she drew in a deep breath. Time to play dumb. "Oh, come on." She pushed out a pouty bottom lip. "I really want a drink." She pushed to her tiptoes and leaned to the side to steal a peeked through the double doors that swung open and closed with the passing guests. "Mr. Green let me in last time. Isn't he here tonight?"

"Yeah, *Raco*. Why don't you ask Mr. Green? I bet he'd be happy to see her."

The bouncer's lip curled. He lowered his clipboard and stepped aside. Malachi grinned and took Tara's hand. "Come on, babe. Let's party."

The laser light show was in full swing. Tara followed Malachi to a side bar—one she hadn't seen the last time she was there. It was narrow and sleek, set up at the back of the room, far from the main dance floor. He pulled out a chair. "Have a seat."

Tara obeyed, though her eyes and ears were wide open. Her hands trembled, and she pulled them into her lap.

The bartender's thin fingers loitered lifelessly on the bar top. He examined her and Malachi, his beady eyes bloodshot and red. "I heard you got snuffed out."

Tara leaned back in her chair, trying not to look like she knew exactly what he was talking about. A knife in the chest would snuff out anyone. Well, almost anyone.

Malachi gestured to Tara. "I think my lady friend here would like a drink."

She perked up. "One of those fizzy drink things I had last time would be awesome." She bobbed her foot to the beat. It was all she could do to block the nerves creeping up her spine.

The bartender popped open a bottle and set it in front of her. He leaned forward on the counter, inspecting Malachi while his fingers tapped on the marble surface. "Mr. Green know you're here?"

"Probably not. I'm hoping to be a pleasant surprise."

"You made it." Andrei paid no attention to Malachi as he stopped beside Tara.

She pivoted the tall barstool. "Yeah, I decided to have one last hurrah before I left."

"Very good." He gestured to her drink. "Is that yours?"

She nodded.

"You take it, and we will go upstairs. VIP level."

Tara clung to Malachi. "What about my friend? Can he come too?"

Andrei didn't give the courtesy of offering a reply. "Get your drink. We go now."

Malachi grabbed her arm. "I believe she's with me. Why don't you tell Mr. Green that I'm back, and I've brought him a gift as a show of good favor?"

Tara stood and rested her hand on her hip, her head cocked to the side—universal dumb girl stance. "What are you talking about?"

Malachi draped his arm over Tara's shoulder. "You're making my date uncomfortable, Andrei. Be a good boy and do as you're told."

The bulky Russian clenched his fists and stepped forward. The air thickened with tension. If she didn't get past this stage, she'd never get upstairs with Malachi by her side, and he was the only protection she had.

She let out a deep sigh. "Okay, well, I guess I'll just take off." She squirmed out from under Malachi's arm. "I *thought* I came to party. So far, this has been a total drag. I'll see you guys later."

Andrei moved in front of her. "Not necessary." He glared over her head at Malachi. "Your friend can come, if it makes you happy, pet."

She smiled, but under her facade, the little voice in the back of her mind was screaming at her to run. "Oh. Okay. That's cool." Tara wrapped her arm around Malachi's. She had to act like his date, but if it didn't look real, Andrei might become suspicious. "VIP level, here we come."

They gathered into a nearby elevator and waited while it ascended. The door slid open and Tara stepped out onto the cherry hardwood floor. Chandeliers dangled overhead, casting soft light throughout the upper level. The elevator doors closed almost silently behind them, trapping them in the quiet space.

Malachi grabbed her arm with a firm hold. Usually that would piss her off, but under the circumstances it was good to know he was close by.

A sleek, low-lying couch hosted two men. One of them Tara recognized, the other had lightly bronzed skin and a pair of glasses perched on the tip of his thin nose.

Mr. Green stood. "Hello, Malachi. I'm happy to see you made a quick recovery." He gestured to the sitting area. "Please, sit."

Tara lowered onto the couch. The fear she had managed to suppress to this point crawled slowly up her legs, prickling her skin. The room was secure and separate from the bottom party level. Even if she wanted to run, there was nowhere to go.

Tiny pink pills were scattered over the surface of a glass coffee table. The empty product bag hung limp over the corner with a scale sitting beside it.

"You're just in time to sample the new shipment," said the other man in a foreign accent. He used a pen to slide two pills toward her. "Ladies first."

She shifted her weight. They looked like the same pills Andrei gave her, but this time each had a bold stamp in white—D5. "What is it?"

"It's a complementary taste." Mr. Green sat back in the couch. "Go ahead. Try it."

She turned to Malachi for reassurance. Taking the pills was the first step of their plan. Then she'd have five hours before she crashed. Five hours to push down the nausea building in her gut, and to dance out the electricity crawling under her skin.

Malachi nudged her and snapped her out of her thoughts. "It's good stuff, love."

She plucked the pills off the table and rolled them into her palm. Her gaze moved from the drugs, to Mr. Green, and then to the man sitting beside him. "If you don't mind me asking, who are you?"

"This," Mr. Green replied, "is a dear friend of

mine who traveled all the way from Japan to visit me. He just happened to come with a gift."

The thin man bowed his head, and the corner of his mouth arched in a grin. "My name is Mr. Yamamoto. A pleasure to meet you." He watched her for a moment longer before his gaze moved to Malachi. "You have a lovely guest. Most women in Japan have jet black hair and olive skin." He sat quietly for a moment, his gaze returning to her face. "It is rare to find a natural beauty with both fiery red hair and porcelain skin in one decadent package."

Tara shifted again. He was sizing her up—inspecting her for whatever purpose she would serve.

Malachi gave a single nod, signaling for her to follow through.

She held her breath. Showtime.

Tara dropped the pills onto her tongue and swallowed them down with a swig of her drink. She glanced at the clock on the wall. Ten o'clock. It would be three o'clock when she crashed. Five hours to consult with Malachi and make sure everything would go as planned.

Mr. Green stole a peek at his watch. "I think you'll like this new product."

She grabbed Malachi's arm. "*New* product?" Clinging to him was all she could do to not jump out of her seat. *New* was not part of the plan. "You said it's a new shipment, now a new product."

Malachi pulled away from Tara and gestured to the Japanese man. "Mr. Yamamoto is our pharmaceutical engineer. This is the new and *improved* Drop5."

Mr. Yamamoto's slanted eyes narrowed even farther, as if he were assessing her reaction. "How do you feel? Dizziness? Fatigue? Muscle cramping?"

"What are you talking about?" Her heart pounded so hard in her chest, she wondered if everyone in the room could hear it over the pulsing music below them. Her gaze flickered from Mr. Yamamoto to Malachi, and back to Mr. Green.

"It is not working," Andrei stated. She'd nearly forgotten he was there, standing quietly against the wall behind her.

Tara turned to Malachi and opened her mouth to tell him their code phrase—the one sentence they agreed would mean to cut and run. But suddenly, she couldn't remember what it was. In fact, she couldn't remember a lot of things. Her gaze slowly dragged across the room. The sparkling chandeliers blurred, looking like clouds of diamonds.

"Ah." Mr. Yamamoto sat back with a pleased expression. "There is the initial reaction." He used the pen as a pointer while he spoke. "You see, her pupils are dilating. Right now she is experiencing confusion. That is designed to keep them cooperative during the transport; much easier than the last Drop5, which gave the unexpected burst of energy first."

She tried to remind herself this was still part of the plan—being taken where only the women could go, deep into the system. And Malachi would be there to protect her. She groped for a hold on his arm but found nothing except the soft fabric of the couch.

"Sorry, Tara." Malachi crossed his arms over his chest, standing with a sadistic grin. "I had to get back in somehow, and delivering the guardian's best friend was my golden ticket. Sarian's pretty pissed you got away last time with that whole time bending escapade. This will definitely earn me brownie points." He bent to tuck a curl behind her ear. She shrugged away. He looked at Mr. Yamamoto. "How long?"

"From start to end, five minutes." He tapped his pen against his leg. "Now, maybe two. See, unlike the other drug, this one is used for quick transport when it's necessary to take the target immediately. But unlike any other drug on the market, this leaves no trace elements in the blood. That is very important. The blood must be pure."

Tara stared up at Malachi with wide eyes. Her gut slithered and she pushed down the urge scream. She had to get out—now. Her attention turned to the elevator doors. She tried to stand, but there was no strength left in her legs. With clouded vision, she reached into her pocket. Her fingers fumbled over the curves of her cell phone.

Malachi snatched it out of her hand and snickered. "You really are naive, Tara."

Images of Peter and his beautiful blue eyes flashed behind her fluttering eyelids. "But what you said—"

"Was all a lie."

CHAPTER NINE

Vines crawled up her inner torso and wove between the gaps of her ribs. The pain wasn't as bad as the raw terror of something slithering inside her. She clenched her jaw, unable to move, trapped, and helpless. The vines deepened their hold, rooting into her, and—to her horror—they began to feed.

Cries from neighboring cells echoed through the halls. Moments later, the heavy metal door creaked open and Sarian strode in, placing one careful step in front of the other to avoid damaging the writhing roots, though they seemed to move out of his way while he crossed the room.

As its thorns moved deeper, she couldn't hold in an exhausted sob. Something told her she wasn't even close to prepared for whatever he was going to do next. Hopefully, he'd become frustrated enough to just get this over with, but she might have to help it along—piss him off enough to make him put her out of her misery.

That was the new plan.

With his cane to assist him in limping toward her, he wasn't dressed in the normal tailored suit he usually wore. Instead, he sported an old style suit with a stripe running down the outside of each pant leg, a single button jacket layered over a collared shirt and a vest, with a top hat perched on his head.

The roots stilled when he stopped in front of her. His grip on the brass handle of his cane tightened. "I am running out of patience and time." With a firm tug, he grabbed what was left of her hair and jerked back her head. "Tell me how to break the obedience spell, and I will command the tree to release you. Refuse…and I will allow it to feed."

"I told you—" She swallowed, peering deep into his black eyes. "I don't know anything about an obedie—"

"You must know something. You are the young guardian's closest ally. She has told you something, anything." His grip on her hair tightened.

She drew in a quivering breath, still glaring up at him. If pissing him off was the last thing she did before she died, that would bring her enough satisfaction to let go of life and move on. Zanya would stay safe, and she'd be free. It was too late for her anyway. Even if he ordered the tree to pull away, her injuries would eventually lead her to the same fate.

"Fine." Her words scratched out of her throat in a raspy whisper. "I'll tell you what you need to hear."

He slowly released her hair, planted one hand on either side of her chair, and towered over her. "Speak."

Her vision focused and she noticed a patch sewn onto the shoulder of his coat, half hidden beneath the extravagant collar. Burgundy and white with highlights of gold, the crest showed two lions perched on either side of a symbol. The big cats sat proud and lean with their golden manes framing their statuesque features. Bright golden eyes stared at her, while folds of a burgundy sash wove around the animal's paws. She peered at it for a moment, examining what looked like an old family crest on a flag.

The vines inside her squirmed, forcing her to shut her eyes and gasp.

"I suggest you hurry, you foolish girl."

She peered through blurred vision and crinkled her nose. "All right. Here it goes." She locked eyes with him one last time. "You really, really need to shower, because you stink to high heaven." His face tightened. "Like, really bad. Rotten egg bad." His lips pursed, and his eyes flooded with violet light, churning like angry waves. "And your clothes are really out of date—" Her remark was cut off with vines tearing through her gut. She moaned. "So there it is. You really, really needed to hear that."

Sarian stood and straightened his jacket. Silently he turned and limped toward the door. On the threshold, he paused. "I will break the obedience spell, with or without your assistance. When I do, your death will have been in vain. I have great plans for the middleworld, but your guardian is making the process difficult. Perhaps losing her closest friend will bring to her attention the desperation of the situation."

Tara didn't have the freedom to inhale without the tree tightening even farther. She waited for a moment while the writhing vines slowly lessened her ability to breathe.

He growled, from deep in his chest, and slammed the door shut. Peering through the metal bars, his eyes slanted up, as if he were smiling. "Let us see where your clever comments have gotten you, shall we?"

***

Tara's eyes shot open. She sat up quickly, to discover her arms tied in front of her with thin rope. A streak of terror arched through her chest, slightly dimmed by the realization she wasn't bound to the chair anymore.

Unfortunately, her position hadn't greatly improved. She scanned a dark basement—or what she assumed was a basement, considering the cement walls and stench of mold, among other foul odors.

"Hello?" She managed to push herself to her feet. "Is anyone in here?

"Shh!" Fingers fumbled against her leg and tugged on her pants. "Sit down," a girl whispered. "Before they come back and see you're standing up."

Tara lowered herself to the floor. "Where are we?"

"Shut up," snapped another, older sounding voice from somewhere to her right.

Tara startled and searched the pitch-black space. She inhaled the stink of sweat and urine, and what she could only identify as old food. Random scratches, coughs, and gentle whimpers came from every direction. "How many people are here? Where are we?"

The younger voice beside her whispered. "I'm Amy. There are lots of people here, so be quiet before you get them mad at all of us cuz you're talking."

Tara quieted and tried to process what had happened.

She must have missed the transportation stage while she was passed out. And she wasn't at all in control of the situation, unlike the plan. She ground her teeth.

Malachi. He'd stabbed her in the back. She pulled her knees to her chest. This was her fault for falling for his story. She'd trusted him after seeing the raw pain in his eyes. All too familiar with that same torment, she'd jumped at the chance to save someone else from ending up as screwed up as her.

Someone coughed, and from the other side of the room there was a sob. There must have been a dozen girls around her, but it was impossible to tell without any light. With her hands tied together, she managed to search her pockets one at a time. *Shit*. Malachi had taken her phone.

She hung her head. There had to be someone who knew more than she did. "Does anyone in here know where we are?" Tara asked in a hushed voice.

"Shh."

Tara glanced around. "We have to try to get out of here."

"They'll kill us," a voice from the far end of the room said with more conviction than Tara expected.

"Some of the girls have already gone missing."

"Missing isn't the right word," another girl said. "Jesus. The screams…"

A door at the top of a tall staircase swung open, casting light into the room. Tara squinted up at the silhouetted figure slowly descending with something in his hands.

Several of the girls began to cry. The light in the room lifted the veil of darkness from not a dozen, but nearly fifty prisoners as far as Tara could estimate. They sat shoulder-to-shoulder, back-to-back, and leaning against each other, all dirty and terrified.

"Hungry?" Tara watched Malachi crouch with a tray of food.

He froze when he noticed the girl lying beside her. A tremble in his hands caused the items on the tray to shake, and the glass of water tilted over and spilled half its contents onto the floor. He set down the tray and slowly reached out to touch Amy. The girl curled into a ball and covered her face.

Tara pushed onto her knees and forced herself between them. She wouldn't let him scare her. The poor girl was terrified enough already.

"You're a damn liar."

He quickly recoiled any obvious signs of remorse and lifted a sandwich to Tara's lips. "Eat this."

She turned her head.

"If she doesn't want it, I'll eat it," Amy whispered. Matted brown hair hugged her cheeks, framing her large brown eyes. She licked her lips. "I'm hungry."

Tara's heart tore. "How long have you kept everyone down here?"

When he set down the food, it was an opportunity she couldn't waste. Tara swung her fisted hands and punched Malachi in the mouth.

He fell back, flipping the tray. "Damn it, Tara. Knock it off. You're wasting your energy." He righted himself and picked up the sandwich. He didn't have the slightest mark on him.

"I trusted you," she whispered, trying not to let anyone else hear. She'd gotten herself into something she may never get out of. She may never see Zanya again, never see Peter. Oh God—Peter. He'd think she just ran away.

"You can't trust anyone. Especially not me." He lifted the sandwich to Tara's lips. "Eat. You'll need your strength for when you guys are moved."

"What about water?" Amy asked—begged.

"All right, honey." Tara pushed hair out of the girl's eyes. "I know you're scared."

She whimpered. "I want to go home."

Tara peered at Malachi. "Can you at least get her water?"

Another girl sobbed, and this time, Tara saw her—a blonde teen, huddled against the wall with blood-matted hair. "Good God. What did they do to her?" A row of deep gashes ran down her legs, poorly bandaged with gauze.

"I told you. A woman's offering is more valuable than boys. Bloodletting. I guess he needed a quick fix." He shoved the food in her face. "Now eat or you'll be hungry for the next few days."

Tara gasped. "Days? Is that how long it's been

since they've eaten?" She stared down at Amy curled up on the floor. "She's so young."

"She's eleven," he mumbled, and shoved the sandwich back in her face. "Now eat."

Tara's stomach twisted in knots. She shook her head. "Go get more water. Tell them I spilled it on accident."

He grabbed her wrists and yanked her forward with a fierce glare. "I don't take orders from anyone." He shoved her back onto the cold concrete. Malachi's tense features relaxed. He gazed down at the girl. "Don't worry. I won't let her die. That'll be one less sacrifice. The boss will be pissed." Malachi picked up the tray and stood.

Tara reached out and took the sandwich, her wrists aching from the tightly wound rope. She lay on her side and pressed the bread and turkey to Amy's lips. "Eat something," she whispered. "Just a bite."

Without hesitation the girl did, and chewed like a hungry animal.

"I want some," one of the prisoners shrieked. "I haven't eaten in two days."

The rest of the group buzzed franticly. Cries and shouts filled the room, bouncing off the cement walls, assaulting Tara from every direction.

Malachi pulled the gun from the back of his pants. "Everybody shut up."

The room instantly fell silent.

He tucked away his weapon and hovered over Amy. "Is she all right?"

Tara glanced up at him. "You have no right to ask that."

He picked up the glass and walked to the bottom of the stairs. "I'll be right back."

Malachi made another water run, and this time brought some for Amy, and some of the other girls, too. Tara gave her drink to a young brunette and instructed her to take just a few sips before passing it down. The water was only enough for a few people but it was better than nothing. She wouldn't risk asking Malachi for more.

Everyone was bound in one way or another. Some of the girls—probably those who had been caught talking—had gags in their mouths. Those who had tried to run had their feet and hands tied, some with raw blisters from the harsh rope. The smart ones, who had stayed quiet and cooperative, had only their hands tied in front of them.

The stench grew stronger by the minute. There was no toilet in the room—only a bucket, which looked as if it had been full for days—sat in a corner.

Heavy boots thumped down the creaking steps. Tara examined the silhouette, larger and bulkier than Malachi's. She curled into a ball, trying to blend with the others as much as possible, which was a hard thing to do when her hair acted like a beacon.

She buried her face between her knees and held her breath, listening to the footsteps grow louder before they stopped. The loud click of a cocked rifle made everyone in the room jump, including Tara. The tingle of fear prickled her skin.

"Stand up," ordered a familiar, thick Russian accent. Everyone remained frozen in place until a massive blast tore through the room, spitting shards of cement in every direction. With a chorus of screams, the girls scrambled to their feet. Andrei gestured to the staircase with the barrel of his rifle. "Get in a line and go up the stairs. Now!" Tara found Amy and grabbed the back of her shirt. They fell into line and marched single file toward the open door, where two more armed guards waited.

Andrei followed the stragglers from the back with his gun aimed while he stood guard. Tara followed Amy through a bare living room with only a subfloor under their feet. The entire house stank of cat urine and mold.

Tara stepped out the front door and into the sunlight, squinting at the gravel driveway. Her eyes ached from the sudden change. Trees and tall weeds surrounded them. It was obvious nobody had lived in that house for a long time.

Tara climbed onto a bus parked in the gravel driveway and picked a seat at the back beside Amy, who hadn't said a word since she'd asked for food. Now that they were out of the basement, it became clear what kind of condition the girl was really in. Dry blood stained her hair and cheek from a gash on her forehead. Her face was pale, and her lips were cracked and dry.

Andrei stood at the front of the bus, holding the gun in clear sight. As the last of the group was forced into seats, Andrei cocked the rifle back a second time, demanding everyone's attention. "We go through town now. If any of you say a word, I will kill you. If you scream, I will kill you. If you—"

"I'm pretty sure they get the point." Tara's head popped up at the sound of Malachi's voice. Without making eye contact with her, he took a seat behind the driver's chair. The burly Russian started the bus and the doors swung shut, followed by the hiss of hydraulics.

It was smart. A school bus filled with young girls wouldn't attract any attention. If a cop were to cruise by, he wouldn't even take a second look.

Amy slowly laid her head down in Tara's lap. "Where are they taking us?"

"I don't know." She stroked the girl's hair, doing what she could to comfort her. "How ya doing, kiddo?"

"Okay," she whispered in a forced breath. "I'm not feeling good, though. My chest hurts. I have asthma."

"Yeah? Well, just take deep breaths." Tara didn't know the first thing about asthma, and if Amy had an attack, there was no way Andrei would bring her to a doctor. He'd probably just kill her on the spot. Some small talk might comfort her. Tara combed her fingers through Amy's knotted hair. "Where are you from?"

"The United States. Montana."

"Really? How did you get so far away from home?"

Amy shivered and curled into a tighter ball. "Vacation. Me and my family came to visit my brother for winter break. He's here on a student exchange program."

If she had a brother and family here in Moscow, maybe they could figure out a way to reach them and get help. She leaned down closer to Amy's ear and whispered. "Do you know how to get a hold of your family?"

"No," Amy whispered in response. "Our cell phones don't work here."

"What about your brother's school?"

She shook her head. "That's where I was taken. My brother fought with the guy who brought you food." A sob trickled from her throat. "My brother tried to protect me."

"Wait a second." She peered at Malachi. "The guy with the dark hair and gauged earrings? *He's* the one who took you?"

She nodded. "I screamed when he grabbed my arm, and my brother tried to push him off."

The news.

Amy was the girl who had been abducted from the private school, and her brother—oh God—her brother was the one who had died. Tara looked back at Malachi's. He must be the gang member brought to the hospital in critical condition. Her stomach rolled.

It all made sense now. This was why everyone was so shocked to see him—why they thought he'd been "snuffed out."

Malachi wasn't a good guy who made some bad choices. He was the worst—a recruiter, and she'd fallen for his act. Tara hung her head, anger wringing her muscles tighter. He'd played her, and now she was stuck.

She drew in a deep breath and stroked Amy's arm. It was a small gesture, but it was all she could do to comfort the poor thing.

Worse, even if they were rescued before becoming Sarian's sacrifices, most of the girls would end up like Tara, having a part of themselves stolen. A part they'd never get back. Not ever. No matter how much they wanted it, cried over it, hurt for it.

Malachi or not, Tara couldn't let these girls be taken away from their families. She had to do something to help them get back to their lives.

Tara glanced down at Amy, who had fallen asleep. Maybe some rest would do her good. There was no telling where they were going, or what would happen once they arrived.

After what seemed like hours later, the bus cruised through a wooded neighborhood with smooth, white sidewalks and cast iron flowerpots hanging from antique looking street lamps. The homes were few and far between, sometimes a mile apart. Residents jogged in high-end sneakers with purebreds trotting beside them. Kids rode tricycles while their mothers pushed three-wheeled strollers.

This had to be the last place anyone would suspect something like this was happening.

The bus made a wide left turn into a smooth driveway that stretched nearly a quarter mile from the road. A brick wall encompassed the property, which was surrounded by more thick forest, making the street almost impossible to see.

A sloping roof with wide eaves topped the sleek exterior of the house. Weeping willow trees and what could only be described as really big bonsai trees were strategically placed around the property, shading a rock garden lying beside the forest.

The bus hissed to a stop and Malachi stood. When his gaze met Tara's, he paused for only a split second before turning toward Andrei.

He didn't give her the courtesy of looking regretful—not even for a moment.

"Get up and go inside," Andrei said, ushering everyone down the stairs of the bus.

Tara shook Amy by the shoulders. "Wake up." The girl moaned, but didn't move. Tara tried to pull her to a sitting position, but with her wrists still bound together, she didn't have the leverage.

"What's going on?" Andrei watched them from the front of the bus.

"I'm trying to wake her up." Tara grunted under the girl's weight. Andrei stomped toward them, gun in hand. "Oh God." She shot to her feet and shielded Amy, but he shoved her aside like she was a feather and grabbed Amy by her hair. A shrill scream ratcheted through the bus. "I said, get up." Andrei threw Amy to the floor. Her forehead smacked against the ridged surface.

Malachi walked toward them and scooped Amy into his arms. He cradled her with tenderness, as if he actually cared about her. He swept hair off her pale cheek, streaking blood over his fingers. He glared up at the Russian.

Andrei jabbed Amy in her ribs with the barrel of his gun. "She's sick. We should do it now."

Tara gasped. "No!"

Malachi grabbed the barrel of the weapon with one hand and tore it from Andrei's grip. Propping Amy against his shoulder, he aimed the gun and curled his finger around the trigger.

Andrei stood silently, his gaze flickering from the polished steel to Malachi's infuriated gaze. "If you touch her again," Malachi snarled, "I won't need this piece of shit gun to put you down."

CHAPTER TEN

Tara followed Malachi down the bus steps and onto the paved driveway. She wasn't going to let Amy out of her sight, especially now that Andrei intended to kill her if he got the chance.

The other girls were already gone, ushered out long before she stepped off the bus. Tara nearly tripped over herself when Andrei jerked her to the right. He was strong. Every movement, even if it was small, threw her around like a rag-doll.

Cars rushed down the residential street and a dog barked from a distant neighbor's yard. They weren't just sounds, they were hope—people lived in those houses, drove those cars, walked those dogs. All of them probably carried a cell phone. A way to get help.

It would take some fancy footwork to reach the brick wall before Andrei caught up to her, and it was a slim chance she'd be able to outrun him, if she could escape his iron grip at all.

She glanced back at Malachi, who walked down a path leading to some kind of tornado shelter at the end of a walkway.

Malachi noticed Andrei force her in the opposite direction. "Hey," Malachi called out, Amy still cradled in his arms. "Where are you taking her?"

Andrei gestured at the house as he continued walking. The fear in Malachi's eyes sent a streak of panic through Tara. She dragged her feet, doing whatever she could to slow down their pace.

"Wait," Malachi shouted. He walked toward them. Tara stumbled, this time on purpose, but Andrei didn't even flinch. His muscles bulged when he pulled her to her feet and continued to drag her forward.

"I said hold up," Malachi shouted again, this time with more irritation in his tone. He broke into a jog while hugging Amy tightly against his chest. The girl squinted at the sun. At least she was conscious.

Finally, Andrei paused and pivoted toward Malachi. "I take the girl to Boss, and you take *that* girl where she belongs." His accent was even thicker when he was angry.

Malachi's lips parted and he glanced at the house. "The boss is here?"

"And he wants *this* girl first." Andrei tugged Tara's arm again, causing the muscle under his grip to throb. She squirmed, but his grip only tightened.

Malachi nodded. "Fine. I'll take her."

"With that sick one?" He scoffed. "You are not bringing that girl to Boss."

Malachi's gaze rested on Amy.

Why did he care so much about a girl he helped kidnap? Unless he felt guilty. Maybe that was it. She straightened her posture, studying Malachi's face. Maybe he actually felt bad for dragging her, and that poor girl, into this mess. It would be the least he could do.

"You're right," Malachi responded. After a moment of hesitation, he extended her to Andrei. "You take this one. I'll bring the redhead to the boss."

So much for that theory.

Tara's entire body jerked back when Andrei pulled her behind him. "Why would I let you take this one?"

Malachi paused. "Because deep down, you're really just a nice guy who wants to be loved?" When Andrei didn't show a hint of amusement, Malachi laid Amy on the shaded ground against the trunk of a tree.

Crouching beside the paling girl, he ran the back of his fingers along her forehead, down her temple, and over the curve of her cheek. Amy cringed and turned her face away. Malachi fisted his hand and pulled it back to his body.

"I'm sorry," he said gently, still focused on the girl. When he stood, his eyes were sharp and the black around them had darkened. "I am going to take the redhead, and you're going to let me, or you'll end up just like your friends—the ones who tried to take her the first time."

Andrei's grip tightened, turning his fingers white with pressure.

"I know you heard about what they found," Malachi said in a warning tone. He took a step forward. "The blood on the ground, and all that was left of your friends in the alley." Twigs cracked under Malachi's soles as he eased toward them.

Andrei swallowed. "I knew there was something wrong with you. Mr. Green saw you die."

Malachi grinned. "He *thought* he saw me die."

"You were in the hospital after they took the girl, and then you were stabbed in the chest. But you came back. You came back both times without a scratch."

Malachi inched forward. He was getting that look again, the gleam in his eye he'd had before he attacked those men in the alley.

Andrei's grip loosened for the first time since they'd gotten off the bus. She craned her neck and stared at the woods lining the brick wall—the only thing separating her from the rest of the world. The populated street was in the distance, and barely visible through the scattered trees, but it was there.

She turned her attention back to the scene at hand. The shadows on Malachi's face spread as if death itself peered from behind his eyes. "Now, give me the redhead, and I'll bring her to the boss."

Andrei's grip loosened even more.

Her heart pounded in anticipation for what would have to be an epic marathon to the brick wall. She readied her legs, drew in a deep breath and, with a burst of adrenaline, tore her arm out of Andrei's grip and sprinted through the yard.

There was no looking back. That would only slow her down. Each frantic stride carried her that much closer to freedom.

She ran toward the woods, and the textured brick beyond that. It was so close. Her instincts got the better of her and she glanced over her shoulder.

Andrei's contorted face loomed mere feet behind her, and she jumped as the panic arched through every muscle in her body.

A shove between her shoulder blades sent her catapulting to the ground with only her extended forearms to break her fall. A loud crack vibrated in her ears when her head smacked against the ground.

"You little bitch." Andrei panted and pulled her to her feet with a single hand. His hot breath broke over her neck. "You want to try to run?" A solid punch to her gut sent her crumbling to her knees. She coughed and wheezed. He grabbed her by her hair and pulled her to her feet for a second time. Even with blurred vision, she could see Malachi marching toward them. Her spark of hope was met with another blow, this time a back handed lap to her cheek that spun her in a half-circle and threw her to the ground.

With her face pressed against the earth, she forced open her eyes. Malachi stood just yards away.

The sound of metal scraping against Andrei's belt buckle made Tara flinch. He pulled her up by her arm. She caught a glimpse of a gleaming blade. It seemed larger than she remembered. Or maybe the fact it was inches from her throat made it a whole hell of a lot scarier.

Her stomach twisted in knots, and she felt her eye begin to swell. In the core of her heart she yearned for Peter's gentle embrace and the sweet smell of freshly fallen rain. She wanted to hear Zanya's quirky giggles and see her shy smile, and get the kind of hug only her best friend could give.

She just wanted to be home with the people who loved her.

But none of that made a difference when the edge of the sharp blade kissed the delicate skin of her throat. Thick fingers spread around her chin and lifted her head, forcing her eyes to the sky. She shrieked in panic, fighting against every urge to pull away. One wrong move would end her with a slit throat. Very carefully, she strained her eyes to look in front of her.

Malachi fisted his hands. "Let. Her. Go."

"You want her?" Andrei tightened his grip, and the blade pressed closer to Tara's skin. Even though she tried not to, she swallowed. Her skin lit on fire with a nick from the blade. "I don't know why you want her, but I will kill her first."

"You really want to know why?" Malachi said in a teasing tone as he took a step forward. His gaze met Tara's, and a grin played over his lips. "Because the party can't start until a redhead's in the room."

It took every ounce of strength for Tara to keep her knees from buckling. She'd thought it was stupid the first time he said it—the code phrase for them to cut and run—but it was perfect for a club setting, so she went with it.

When he gave a reassuring nod, she knew. Even after all that had happened, Malachi hadn't abandoned her.

The grinding of Andrei's teeth scraped along Tara's eardrums. She gasped when he shoved her to the ground and then charged after Malachi with the blade raised above his head. Malachi waited until the last second, then ducked and collided with Andrei's knees. The towering Russian flipped over his head and landed on his back with a loud thud and a wheeze.

Tara used all of her strength to stand, but only managed to stay upright by swaying like a drunkard.

Andrei turned onto his belly and pushed onto his hands and knees. Malachi grabbed his adversary's hand and twisted it, sending the blade clattering to the paved driveway.

"You have a real problem with touching little girls, don't you, *Andrei*." The loud snap of the man's wrist cued a scream, which was quickly silenced by a blunt punch to his jaw. Andrei collapsed flat against the ground. "I told you I wouldn't need the gun to put you down."

Tara scanned the grounds and spotted Amy, still slumped against the tree. She ran toward her, stumbling along the way, until she fell onto the mulch beside her. Pale cheeks and dusky lips masked the girl's once rosy features.

The girl struggled to breathe. The raspy inhales and wheezing exhales sounded like she was having an asthma attack. "Do you have any medicine?" Though barely noticeable, the girl nodded and leaned to the side. Tara slipped her fingers into the back pocket of Amy's jeans and found an inhaler. "I—" She flipped the inhaler on either side, searching for instructions. "I don't know how to use this thing."

A hand rested on Tara's shoulder. Malachi grabbed her forearm, Andrei's knife clenched in his other hand. "Hold still." He sliced through the rope binding her wrists, finally setting her free. The skin on her wrists sighed with relief when the cool air caressed the swollen marks.

Malachi grabbed the inhaler and fell to his knees beside Amy. He shook the cartridge, slipped the mouthpiece between her lips and pressed on the top. A sharp blast of medicine pushed into her lungs as she inhaled. Amy nodded, and Malachi gave her another dose. "Sit up." He picked her slumped body from the base of the tree and straightened her back. "Remember what Mom always said. Breathe in through your nose, and out through your mouth, like you're blowing bubbles." He mimicked the process, his stomach puffing out with every inhale, and the exhale passing through the soft O of his lips.

Amy strained to look at him with her big brown eyes. The wheezing hadn't stopped, but the flush had returned to her cheeks. She caught her breath enough to speak. "How do you know—?"

Her words were cut off with a labored breath.

"Don't worry about that right now. You're doing great," he reassured her. "Once. Twice." She followed his coaching. "That's good. You're doing awesome."

Tara stood up, rubbing her tender wrists. She dabbed at the sticky blood on her neck and winced when her fingers brushed against the tiny cut. She was lucky she hadn't gotten her throat sliced wide open, and had Malachi to thank for it.

Tara froze. "The other girls. Where are they?" Malachi gestured to the slanted doors of what she assumed was an underground tornado shelter nestled beside a storage shed. She ran toward them, and moments later, Malachi matched her pace. Tara glanced at him. "Where's Amy?"

"I left her in the shade. She needs to rest."

"Fine. We have to get those girls out of here. Right now."

Malachi grabbed her arm. "No, we can't. The boss is in that house, and stopping *him* is the only way we'll really help." He ran his fingers through his hair. "Listen. We're lucky he hasn't realized anything's gone wrong, but if someone doesn't come knocking on his door with a first class delivery, he'll know, and there will be no way we can save those girls after that."

He stopped talking when Tara tightened her jaw. His gaze locked with hers, and his shoulders slumped forward. "Look at you." He brushed his finger softly along her temple near her eye, now swollen half shut. "I didn't mean for you to get hurt. I swear. I just needed you to believe it, or they wouldn't have believed it, and everything would have fallen apart."

She slapped his hand away. "I don't care what your reasons are, but you owe me some answers. After we finish this, you're going to give them to me. That's the deal. Take it or leave it."

"You'll have answers." He reached into his pocket and pulled out her cell phone. "I've already made sure of that if it's really him in there and the shit hits the fan, you get Amy and run. Understand?"

She snatched her cell phone tried to turn it on, but the battery was dead. She dropped her hand to her side. "Of course."

"Don't worry. I didn't waste the battery for nothing. Now, promise me you'll get Amy out. Even if you can't get the others. Save *her*."

She shoved her cell phone into her pocket. "What is it with you and her anyway? Why do you care about her so much?"

Anguish flooded his gaze. "She's the girl they took—the one I thought I'd never see again. I know this won't make any sense, but…she's my sister."

Tara's lips parted, shocked at first, and then just pissed. "Liar. I know that's not true." She curled her lip into a snarl. "She told me *you* were the one who kidnapped her—tore her away from her brother!" Tara stepped toward him, toe to toe. "Do you know that boy died on the street? Alone. Scared. And now you have the nerve—"

He grabbed her arms. "I know. I was scared as hell, staring up at the dark sky with only the sound of screeching wheels in my ears." He swallowed and loosened his grip. "My sister was gone, and I was alone while blood pooled under my body. The blackness crawled around my vision, sucking me in faster than I was ready to go." His voice caught in his throat. "Then it happened, and there was nothing I could do to stop it."

Her blood pressure spiked. Could it be true? It didn't make sense, but impossible had become a word stricken from her vocabulary. Still, Amy would have recognized her own brother.

He dropped his hands to his sides. "Just…trust me. This one last time."

With little choice, she nodded. "Let's just get

this over with so we can get those girls out of that hole in the ground."

It took them several minutes to reach the main entrance to the house, a large carved door with wooden dragons slithering along the dark trim.

"Remember," Malachi whispered. "Stick close to me." He wrapped his fingers around the heavy brass knocker and slammed it three times.

A soft spurt of static whispered from a speaker mounted beside the door, followed by the subtle voice of a man. "Who is there?"

Malachi leaned toward the speaker. "I'm here with your delivery."

Tara jumped when an electric buzzer sounded, and the heavy lock clicked out of the frame. They glanced at each other before he pushed open the door and peeked inside.

There was nobody there to greet them, and she sensed from Malachi's hesitation that he was nervous. She glanced over her shoulder at the brick wall. It seemed so far away now.

Chapter Eleven

They stepped through the entry on to light bamboo floors, gleaming against the dark wooden shutters and transparent shoji screen doors.

"Hello?" Malachi called out, his muscles tense while he glanced around the open space with clean, sleek lines. Sunlight beamed through the skylights in the ceiling.

"Please, come in and make yourselves comfortable," a man said from another room. His accent was subtle, but eerily familiar. Tara's attention was drawn to the shadow of a man sitting behind one of the screen doors.

"Boss?" Malachi waited for the man to respond.

"Do you have my delivery? I have been eagerly waiting to see her again."

The knots in Tara's stomach pulled tighter. She didn't know what he meant by "again," but if they were going to get close to him, she would have to play along.

Malachi's eyes narrowed, and the darkness around them deepened a shade. Tara still hadn't figured out who, or what, Malachi was *exactly*, but he had promised answers, and she'd have to wait until this was over to get them.

With more confidence than Tara expected, Malachi strutted into the boss's living room. A man sat on a plush floor cushion beside a low-lying table with his back facing them. Steam from hot tea rose above his head, infusing the air with ginger and berries.

He extended his hand. "Please. Come sit."

Malachi's glares choked what little bravery Tara had left. From the raw loathing in his fixed stare, things were going to get ugly—fast.

She stepped back as the boss rose gracefully from the floor. The black sheen of his neatly trimmed hair matched his Japanese house robe, paired with white linen pants that stopped just above his ankles. His bare feet shifted, and he turned to face them.

Mr. Yamamoto returned her stare, and the light smirk that played across his lips vanished. "What happened to her?" he said sharply. "You were to deliver her to me unharmed."

"You should be worrying about yourself right now." The words slithered from Malachi's lips, while the darkness around his eyes deepened to midnight black.

Mr. Yamamoto responded by calmly untying his robe and allowing it to fall from his shoulders. The satin floated to the floor, revealing tattoos that cloaked his body from the collar of his neck to the cuffs of his wrists and vanished below the waistline of his pants. Tara had never seen so many tattoos. She gawked at the painted Japanese warrior driving his samurai sword through a whale swimming across Mr. Yamamoto's chest. Blue waves of ink stretched down his arms in patterns, only interrupted to flow around flames and the rope to a harpoon.

Not wearing his glasses, and with the curves of his lean muscles pushing up the elaborate tattoos, Mr. Yamamoto looked nothing like the frail man at the club where she'd first met him. He appeared to be a gang lord—the kind who ruled with no mercy and gave little regard to human life. Just the sort of man Sarian needed to do his dirty work.

The tattoos that wound around his legs flexed when Mr. Yamamoto bent his knees and took the stance of a warrior.

Malachi gently pushed Tara toward the door, his gaze locked on his opponent. "You're done here. Run."

She nodded and backed away, but when her back met a solid chest, she froze, panic screaming through every nerve.

Thick fingers pressed over Tara's mouth, muffling a shriek. "I want to stay and watch this," Andrei whispered in her ear. "It should be very entertaining."

Her eyes widened when Mr. Yamamoto rushed forward and kicked Malachi square in the chest, sending him flying back. Tara screeched against the hand holding her and tried to break free, but her efforts were met with the coil of muscle in Andrei's arm.

Malachi pushed himself to his feet.

They sprinted toward each other at the same

moment, colliding like two battering rams midair. Yamamoto curled his fingers and used his hardened palm as a weapon, striking Malachi in his face before targeting his chest and torso. A crack sounded when the last of the punches snapped Malachi's rib. He shouted and hunched over, blood dripping from his nose.

Malachi's back rose and fell with every furious breath. He slowly straightened, grinding his teeth as the black over his eyes spread over his face.

Mr. Yamamoto took a step back. It was the first sign of hesitation Tara had seen since they walked in, but it didn't last long. Before Malachi could recover, another attack was underway. Yamamoto grabbed an elaborate sheath displayed on the wall and pulled out a curved sword.

Tara wrapped her hands around Andrei's forearm and struggled to get free. She'd already seen Malachi stabbed in the chest once. She had no desire to see it again.

She froze.

Malachi had been stabbed in the chest…and survived. She had forgotten he was more than the average guy. Malachi straightened up, his fists balled while the black around his eyes grew to nearly covering his face.

The long blade gleamed, displaying something written in Japanese along the curve. Yamamoto gripped the handle of the sword, causing the tendons in his fingers to tighten under his skin. He swiped the blade gracefully through the air in an elaborate figure eight, lowering his stance and carefully positioning his feet on the floor.

They circled each other, one cautious footstep at a time.

"You know there is no hope for you now," Yamamoto said.

Malachi spit a mouthful of blood. "My hope was gone when I died." Yamamoto peered at him, and Malachi charged. The weapon sliced Malachi's gut, splattering blood over his shirt, but it didn't stop him. He jerked the weapon from Yamamoto's grasp and cast it to the ground.

Malachi gripped Yamamoto's neck, not quite strangling him, but holding him still. Malachi parted his lips, and an eerie hissing noise floated out of his throat.

Struggling to breathe, Yamamoto stared into Malachi's changing features. "What are you?" Yamamoto choked.

Malachi raised him into the air with a single hand, cutting off any breath the boss could pull into his lungs.

The darkness slithered from his mouth with his words. "I. Am. Vengeance."

The smell of rot shot up Tara's nose. Andrei let go and stumbled back toward the door. She covered her mouth with her hand. He tripped over furniture, feeling his way along the frail walls, unable to tear his eyes away from the scene.

"I bet it's not so entertaining now," Tara said, watching Andrei over her shoulder. He looked at her, then back to Yamamoto. His face drained of color.

A black cloud poured from Malachi's mouth, invading Yamamoto through his nose and throat.

The shadow seized his muscles. Yamamoto's body convulsed while his face paled and thinned, as if the life were being drained from him bit by bit. Yamamoto's eyes bulged, his cheekbones protruding more as the muscle shriveled under his skin.

Tara screamed and stumbled back, falling to the floor while watching the darkness consume what was left of the gang lord.

Flesh and bone sat in a pile, emitting a stench of carnage.

Her stomach turned, and Tara crawled backward. It was like a train wreck—horrifying, but impossible to look away.

When Malachi turned toward her, the shadows over his face were nearly gone. His eyes saddened, and he glanced at the putrid remains.

Before she could push to her feet, Malachi stalked toward her. Her hands outstretched, she scooted her back against a wall. "Please don't hurt me."

"Tara. Get up. I would never." He reached toward her.

She screamed and slapped him away. "Get away from me!"

He shot her a stern look, then grabbed her and pulled her to her feet. With his hands planted on each side of her face, he stared into her eyes. "There's no time to be delicate about this. My contract is up, and I only have a few minutes left. But trust me when I say this is for your own good. Consider it a gift."

Her eyes widened when his lips parted and the

shadow crept from his mouth. She tried to struggle, but his grip was like iron. The blackness caressed her lips.

CHAPTER TWELVE

Tara's eyes fluttered open. She squinted up at the swaying tree branches overhead. Cherry trees were dotted with pastel petals, gently caressed by a cool breeze.

She drew in a deep breath, tranquility blanketing her mind. If this was death, it was beautiful. A sincere sense of inner peace settled inside her. A tear rolled down her cheek. She smiled softly, the sun beaming through gaps in the branches and onto her face, warming her skin.

Sirens tore through the air, dragging her back to reality.

Groggy, she rolled slowly to her side. Amy lay nearby between two hedges, where Malachi had left her.

Tara pushed onto her hands and knees and crawled toward her. She shook the girl until Amy opened her eyes with an annoyed moan. Tara exhaled and sat beside her.

"What happened?" The raspy words clawed out of Amy's throat.

Tara didn't have the answer. There was nobody

left in the yard, and Malachi wasn't anywhere in sight. With shaky legs, she picked herself off the ground and spotted the wooden cellar doors, still locked shut.

"Stay here. I have to go check on the others."

She dragged each foot across the yard until she reached the doors. Thankfully there was only a wooden broomstick wedged through the handles to keep the doors shut. She grabbed the shaft and slid it out of place.

Tara rubbed her face, her fingers shaking over her lips. God help her. If the girls weren't okay, she'd never forgive herself. She wrapped her fingers around the cold steel handle and heaved open the left door.

Light beamed into the old shelter, highlighting the faces of the group. The girls shielded their eyes, squinting up at her from the corner where they were huddled.

Tara fell to her knees and cradled her face in her hands. A sob pushed out of her chest. They were alive.

The sirens grew louder, and emergency vehicles tore down the long driveway in single file. What must have been a half dozen police cars, followed by a fire truck and two ambulances, skidded to a halt.

The passenger door to a squad car flung open and Peter jumped out, searching the growing crowd of girls who were emerging from the shelter.

Tara jumped to her feet, facing Peter. They locked eyes.

"Tara!" He sprinted toward her. His body

slammed into hers and he threw his arms around her, lifting her off the ground. Peace and light and the scent of freshly fallen rain washed over her like a wave of comfort.

She laid her cheek on his shoulder and, for the first time in a long time, allowed herself to rest.

Peter was there, and all she had to do was *be*.

Be happy.

Be thankful.

Be loved.

This was clearly the place to *be*, and she swore never to forget that again.

***

Tara sat in the hotel restaurant eagerly awaiting a stack of buttermilk pancakes. Fresh coffee steamed from her cup, mixing with the scent of fresh, buttery biscuits.

She tucked a curl behind her ear. It bounced back and sprung against her cheek. Even her hair had returned to its perky self.

Peter reached across the table and put the curl back in its place while she sipped her coffee and took another bite of jam-smothered toast.

"Thanks," she said, still chewing. She swallowed and drank her entire glass of orange juice in one breath. "God, I'm starving." She signaled to the waitress for a refill and took another bite of toast. "I'm sorry you have to see me eating like such a pig."

Peter chuckled. "I'm just glad you're eating again." A grin played across his lips. "I was starting to wonder when you'd put a little weight back on. You were getting too skinny for my taste."

She glanced down at herself. He had a point. She'd lost even more weight during the whole ordeal. It had been a streak of luck to find a pair of pants that still stayed on when she walked. She missed her curves, too. They were part of her. That was clear now, and she loved herself more because of it.

The waitress placed another glass of orange juice on the table, followed by a plate of steaming pancakes. Tara drenched them in a lake of amber syrup before cutting off a bite and folding it into her mouth. After a few bites, she shrugged. "Still not as good as yours."

Peter sat forward and leaned on the table. He slid a black box toward her, and left it sitting beside the cup of coffee.

She stopped chewing. "What's that?" As if she didn't already know. She swallowed her mouthful of pancakes, suddenly not very hungry anymore.

"Just open it."

She sat back and watched him. "You still want to give that to me?"

He arched a brow with a half-crooked grin, which either meant *shut up and kiss me* or *stop asking stupid questions*.

Tara dragged the box toward her. She pried it opened slowly, and stared down into the satin bed. "Um…it's empty."

He reached across the table and laced his fingers with hers. "Listen." He glided his thumb in circles over the top of her hand as he spoke. "I want you to know I love you, and I always will. But that doesn't mean we have to get married if that's not what you want. I don't care. As long as we're together. We can keep taking it slow. I'll wait for you as long as it takes, and if that means putting the physical half of our relationship on hold..." He smiled. "Well, I won't lie. It was exciting..." He leaned in closer. "But you're worth more than that."

Her smile quickly vanished when she recalled her desperate attempt to throw herself at him. She sank into her chair. She pulled her hand away and fidgeted with her fingers. "Yeah. Uh...about that." Her cheeks flushed with heat while she struggled to find the right words. She'd been such an idiot. "I..." She met his gaze, the heat in her cheeks rising. "What I did before everything happened...going to your room like that." She cupped her hands over her face. It was just too embarrassing to go on.

"Tara." His voice seemed closer. She peeked between her fingers to find him on one knee beside her. Everyone in the restaurant silenced.

"Oh. My. God." She dropped hands slipped into her lap. "Peter, please get up." She glanced around at the gawking crowd of people.

"I need to ask you something first." He took her hand, and she could have sworn everyone in the room had stopped breathing. He cleared his throat. "I don't want to marry you."

"What?" She nearly choked on the word.

"I want to be with you. And if that's the only commitment you can make right now, I'll take it." He placed a kiss on the back of her hand. "Tara Weeble, you'd make me the happiest man in the world if you would be mine, forever. No ring. No ceremony. Just love me, and I swear that I will love you. Not only for the rest of your life, but for the rest of mine."

Whatever they'd face, whatever obstacles might lie in front of them, they would work it out together. The issue of her mortality would be something they'd deal with later. But for now, as long as he wanted her, she would be his. She would never be able to be anything else, even if she wanted to. That was clear now.

With a beaming smile, she nodded. "Yes."

A mixture of cheers and claps roared through the restaurant. Peter stood and gathered her in his arms. He buried his nose in her curls and placed a kiss on the curve of her neck.

While the rest of the guests returned to eating their breakfast, Tara relished the feeling of being back where she belonged. The room filled with chatting, clinking of plates and utensils, giggles, whining children, and the hustle of the kitchen.

Out of the corner of her eye, she noticed a woman loitering in the doorway, staring at her. Frail, with shoulder length brown hair that curled at the ends, she laced her fingers in front of her, waiting.

Tara tapped Peter on the shoulder and nodded toward her. He glanced at the woman. "Right on time." Peter stepped aside. "There's someone here who wants to meet you."

Tara took his hand. "Who is she?"

"Let's invite her to join us. I think you'll want to hear what she has to say." Peter waved the woman over.

The lines stamped on the corners of the woman's mouth deepened as she took a seat.

Big brown eyes watched Tara. "I—" The woman's shaky voice caught in her throat. She paused to collect herself. "I'm Laura, Amy's mom."

Tara peered at the woman's aging face. Under the layers of stress lines, the girl's features were there—her wide brown eyes and the curve of her button nose.

"How is she doing?" The last time she saw the girl, the ambulance was carting her away. God forbid her mom came with bad news.

Laura nodded. "Better." She swallowed, wringing her fingers. "The doctors said she came down with an upper respiratory infection. Who knows where they kept her—" Her voice cut off, and tears welled in her eyes. "I didn't ask Amy what happened exactly, but she did tell me that you watched out for her, and I wanted to thank you."

Tara tightened her grip around Peter's hand. "I'm just glad she's okay."

"She wouldn't have been if it weren't for you. Amy's asthma doesn't usually get that bad. She's been wheezing so badly, and I could just imagine how she sounded without the doctors there to help."

The woman's relief pushed through the layers of grief displayed in her features. Laura had also lost her son, and he deserved to be remembered in all of this. She slid her hand across the table to the woman's, and rested her fingers over the top of her wrist. "I'm so sorry for your loss."

Laura's gaze met hers. More tears built until they

slid down her face.

"Amy told me your son did everything he could to save her. He was a true hero."

The woman's shoulders shook and she hung her head. "He was a good boy, and he loved Amy more than anything in the whole world. I still haven't told her that he's gone. I don't know how I'll even manage—"

"He was there—with Amy—the whole time, in spirit. He didn't leave her side until he knew she would be safe. And he's the only reason that she, or any of those girls, got out alive. That's what you can tell her. Tell her to be proud."

Laura checked her watch. "I have to get back to the hospital. My husband is there alone, and he was really shaken up when I left."

"Of course."

The woman stood and, after a short pause, smiled. "Thank you."

Tara nodded. Moments later Laura was gone.

Tara exhaled and sat back in her chair. "I'm really glad Amy is better."

"She was right, you know? You did something pretty amazing by staying with that girl. By staying with all of them when they needed you. They'll never forget that and neither will their families."

"Well, if it wasn't for that caravan of police and—" She paused and sat up in her chair. "Hey, how did you know where to find me, anyway?"

"We followed the signal after you pressed your panic button on your phone. It took us forever to find the place, though."

"Wait." She stared down at her phone sitting on

the table. "The battery was dead when I got it back. Before that I didn't…" She opened her phone and scrolled through her applications. Nothing seemed out of the ordinary. She opened her camera application to browse the photos, but none of her pictures were there anymore. Every snapshot of her and Peter, the sites in Moscow, her and Zanya—gone.

The only file that remained was a single video.

"Uh…" She glanced at Peter. "I'll be right back." She slipped away from the table and snuck into the bathroom. The video might not be pleasant, and she didn't want to panic in front of Peter if it was more than she could handle.

She locked the door and leaned against the cold tile walls. She tapped her finger over the play button.

Malachi pointed the phone at himself. "Hey, Tara." His awkward, crooked grin sent a streak of grief through her heart. She thought of Amy's mother, there just moments ago. Amy's mother, and from what he'd said, his mother, too. "I promised you answers, so here they are." He cleared his throat. "My name is Timothy Woods, and I'm dead. Well, technically, anyway." He rubbed the back of his neck. "You may think I'm a real piece of shit after you watch this, but I did what I had to do to get Amy back. I actually didn't think I'd ever see her again." He sat and adjusted the angle of the camera. "I guess I underestimated the guy who grabbed her. He pulled out a gun and shot me. I was able to get the gun out of his hand. I panicked and shot him back.

"We were both lying there in the street when the car peeled out. It took a while for me to die, and in those last few moments…" He glanced around the room, his features tight. "Fuck. You know, you'll do anything to save someone you love. Even if that means making a deal with the Devil. In this case, a seriously evil bitch named Contessa."

He stared into the camera. "So I did. She said she'd give me one last chance to get Amy back if I stopped them from sacrificing the girls. I had a feeling she had her own agenda, but at the time I didn't care. That landed me in the body of the asshole who was in the hospital. I took over his body, knew what he knew, and understood I could find the son of a bitch who ran this thing, and cut off the head of the snake." He sat silent for a moment, and then shrugged. "That's it."

He stood and picked up the phone, aiming the camera at his face. "So make sure to tell my little sister I love her, and my mom…tell my mom I'm sorry. It's fucked up, leaving them behind like this, but it's worth it. Well, that is if everything works out as planned. I guess we'll see." He flashed a gentle smile. "I wish I could have met the guardian. If she's friends with you, she must be pretty cool…and lucky." He picked up the phone, filming blurry streaks of wall and floor before he focused the camera on his face again. He smiled. "See ya on the other side."

Chapter Thirteen

Wrapped in Peter's arms was exactly where she wanted to be. They lay in his bed, munching on potato chips—no doubt another of his efforts to help her gain a few pounds.

He flipped through the TV channels after the English marathon of *Karate Kid* movies had finished. Peter scanned through each one for a split second, passing over a news station. Tara caught sight of Mr. Yamamoto's house. She jumped, grabbed the remote, and flipped it back.

"Hey—"

"Shh!" She stared wide-eyed at the reporter standing on the smooth driveway with yellow police tape encompassing the home.

"I'm standing in front of the home of a Mr. Katumi Yamamoto, who authorities have confirmed was a Yakuza ring leader from Japan, leading a major human trafficking organization in Moscow."

"So that's what they think it was," Tara whispered. "Makes sense."

"Over ten kilos of an unknown drug has been found in an underground bomb shelter—the same shelter a group of girls were rescued from after police were led to the scene. Unfortunately, according to eye witnesses, not everyone made it out alive."

Tara scooted to the edge of the bed, watching the officers behind the reporter haul out bags from the shelter wrapped in silver tape. K9 officers sniffed the perimeter while other men geared up into biohazard suits.

"The group of men behind us," the reporter said, pointing to the homicide cleanup crew, "have been called in to deal with what authorities could only describe as 'grisly remains.'"

"Jesus," Peter whispered. He scooted beside Tara. "What the hell happened in there?"

Tara slowly shook her head, unsure how to respond. Because when it came down to it, *what* Malachi did to that man was beyond explanation, and what he'd done to her remained to be seen. But she was eating and sleeping again, all without a nightmare or even so much as a hiccup.

Deep down, she knew.

Malachi had torn the grief right out of her, just before he vanished from sight.

The reporter faced the camera, gripping her microphone with both hands. "Although it's not entirely clear what happened, one thing is for sure. A group of innocent girls have been reunited with their families, and the streets are safer with the trafficking operation shut down."

Peter turned off the TV with the remote. "I think that's officially the end of me watching the news. Ever."

Tara giggled and turned toward him. "Why? It was all good news."

"Yeah, this time." He pulled her close. "But it could have turned out a lot different." He brushed his lips against hers, sending a chill down her back. She leaned into him and kissed him deeper, smoothing the tip of her tongue over his.

Her phone rang in her pocket, and she paused.

"Don't answer that," Peter whispered. Tara smiled, his breath caressing her mouth. When the ringing stopped, she wrapped her arms around his neck and stretched out on top of him. His chest moved up and down under hers while he worked his fingers through her curls. His scent washed over her. She drew it in, cherishing the fresh spring air that came with his embrace.

The phone buzzed again, and Tara sat up. "Maybe it's Renato," she said, scooting off the bed. Peter groaned and sat up, watching as she dug in her jacket pocket. She glanced at the number on the phone with the name beside it. "Oh my God, it's Zanya." She answered the call and pressed the phone to her ear. "Hello?" Static buzzed in the microphone for a moment. Then a voice pushed through. Tara's eyes narrowed, listening carefully. "Hello?"

"Hello? Can you hear me?"

Tara gasped. "Zanya!"

Peter shot off the bed.

"Tara! Is Jayden okay? Go check on him. I think he's back. I don't know if you can hear me, but we're coming home. Contessa—" Zanya's voice wove through waves of static.

The call cut off, and Tara pulled the phone away from her ear. She looked at Peter. "We have to go see Jayden. Zanya's on her way."

Peter nodded. "Just give me a second to throw on a shirt."

She gazed out the French doors leading to the balcony. The doors reminded her of Renato's home, and the lights beyond looked the same as the twinkling orbs she'd admired from the office building when she was with Malachi.

"It's funny where life takes you," she said to herself softly. "My life went from miserable, to worse, to free, to lost, and now—"

"I'm ready." Peter softly took her hand, tearing her eyes away from the view. "Come on. We'll go talk to Renato, together." He hugged her and placed a kiss on her temple. "Everything's going to be all right."

He walked toward the door and opened it, then paused. She gazed into his deep blue eyes.

He tilted his head. "Ready?"

Tara nodded and crossed the room with a smile.

With him, she was home.

*****Sneak Peek*****

Find out what happens next in:

LIGHTS OF AURORA

CHAPTER ONE

The scent of dried herbs and fresh rain poured through the open window.

For the rest of her life, with every whiff of sage or wet earth, Zanya's mind would turn back to Contessa's quaint home in Moscow and the shock that had locked her muscles, making her a mere statue in the room.

She might as well have been a statue when it really mattered. Zanya could still see Jayden's bright blue eyes staring back at her while he struggled to hold Sarian off long enough for them all to escape.

She could have saved him if she'd been more focused. More experienced with her abilities. Instead she'd done exactly what Contessa'd thought they'd do all along. Failed. She couldn't even heal Jayden. Not fast enough.

A tear slipped down her cheek, and she tightened her fists as she stared down at Jayden's body. Someone had to care for him. Even though his spirit had been torn from this world, he deserved his last rites.

Zanya exhaled and draped a sheet over his face.

Their mission to retrieve his soul could fail, and the boy she'd first met in the orphanage could be ripped out of her life, leaving an empty hole of memories and regret.

She crouched beside Jayden, placed a kiss on his shrouded forehead, and whispered in his ear. "Hang on. I'm coming for you." She tightened her grip on the cotton sheet. "I'll get you back." Her voice caught in her throat, and she choked back a flood of tears.

Arwan placed his hand on her shoulder. She looked up at him and saw empathy behind his gaze. "We will get him back," Arwan said. The silky tone of his voice usually comforted her, but not now. Not until Jayden was back, alive, and safe. It would happen somehow. She'd make sure of it.

Zanya forced herself to stand. The fabric of her canary-yellow ball gown swooshed with the movement, a badge of blood smeared across the front. Jayden's blood, and somehow that made it worse.

First she needed to get out of her ridiculous dress. She wouldn't be able to hike through the caves of Naj Tunich in a gown.

Uncle Renato's dress shoes tapped over the floor as he approached from behind. "I'm calling Peter." He dialed a number on his phone, stealing the occasional glance at Contessa from the corner of his eye. "I hope he is still at the hotel."

"Make sure you don't tell Tara where we're going," Zanya said. "She'll freak out."

"As she should. This mission of yours may as well be a suicide attempt." He frowned. "The king of the underworld will never allow you to leave there alive." Renato walked outside to Contessa's front step without another word.

He was probably right, but she couldn't turn her back on Jayden when he needed her the most. Suicide mission or not, she was going after him.

Hawa moaned, tearing Zanya's attention away from her thoughts. Hawa lay on Contessa's couch with her leg elevated on a stack of pillows. The break was bad, but she wasn't crying anymore. That was a good sign—even if Contessa had only healed Hawa to make her shut up. The red-haired witch had even had the audacity to say that aloud.

Zanya's stomach twisted.

Renato walked back inside, the corners of his mouth sloped into an even deeper frown. "Peter did not react well to our plans. He insists on going with the two of you. He's coming here right now."

"No, he can't come with us. Tara will already be pissed at me for taking off without telling her. I can't take Peter too."

"Then you should depart as quickly as possible." Renato rested a hand on Arwan's shoulder. "You and I have been friends for many years." Renato nodded a single time. "I know you will take good care of her."

Determination sparked in Arwan's eyes. Zanya didn't doubt what Renato said was true. He would protect her, no matter the cost.

Zanya bit her lip. She was moved he cared so much, but he was risking his life now too.

The cab took nearly an hour to arrive. While the taxi waited by the curb, Zanya stood on Contessa's doorstep. She and Arwan would drive straight to the airport, but first he'd have to come out of Contessa's house. No doubt Renato was giving him every precaution to take before their journey.

She gazed lifelessly at the mud-crusted rims and the fogged taxi light while her mind wandered between realms.

Whispers yanked her out of her thoughts.

You will never recover him. You are a failure, just as your mother was. But I have plans for you, and soon you will be mine.

Zanya narrowed her eyes. She turned and peered over her shoulder, expecting to see someone there— someone she would promptly punch in the face for being such an asshole. But she was alone on the steps.

Was she seriously going crazy?

The blare of the taxi's horn made her jump. It must be the stress, or the fact she had barely slept for the last few days. Deprivation played tricks on the mind.

Renato's voice became louder as he and Arwan walked toward the open door. He handed Arwan a credit card and some cash before they shook hands. The lines on her uncle's face deepened when he turned to her and pulled her into a hug. As he cradled her against his tailored suit, the rich scent of tobacco surrounded her. All of her life she had wished for someone to care about her the way Renato seemed to, though she'd only known him for a short time. Still, his embrace was enough to make her hesitant to say good-bye.

"You must make it out of this journey alive," he said in a raspy whisper. "Even if you do not succeed in retrieving Jayden's spirit, please—" he held her tighter, "—return unharmed."

Zanya nodded and forced a smile. "I'm not planning on dying anytime soon. The stone needs me."

His grip loosened, and he looked down at her, his familiar brown eyes filled with a mixture of despair and pride. "The stone is not the only one who needs you, Zanya."

His fear was well founded. She was about to walk straight to the gates of hell with no knowledge of what to expect.

"Now go," Renato continued. "Go, and come home safely."

"Make sure to tell Tara…" Her throat ached. Damn. She couldn't keep her emotions as hidden as she'd hoped. Leaving her best friend behind was something she'd sworn she'd never do. Not in the orphanage. Not after they were taken away from that place. Not ever. Now she was going against every oath she'd ever made to herself—and to her friend.

Zanya reached into her bag and grabbed the pendant Cualli, the middleworld goddess, had given her. The pendant was a gift and an omen of support, and usually it calmed Zanya.

Arwan lifted a duffle bag from the floor. He traced his fingers down her cheek, holding her gaze until she finally allowed a hint of a true smile to break through. His touch was all he could give to comfort her. Showing him it had worked, even a little, was the least she could do. After all, he insisted on going with her, and there was nothing she could do to repay that.

The cab's horn blared again. Zanya jumped and glared at the taxi. "You'd think he'd be happy to just sit there with the meter running."

Arwan shook Renato's hand one last time. Zanya shifted her weight, her feet rooted to the ground as she contemplated one last hug. When she glanced at her uncle, her eyes stung with more tears. He must have noticed her hesitation. Maybe even understood it.

With a soft smile, Zanya walked straight to the cab without any more good-byes.

***

In the dressing room of the sporting goods store, Zanya checked herself in the mirror, horrified at what she saw. Wet, limp hair stuck to her cheeks and neck. A huge bloodstain spread over the front of her once-beautiful gown, which was now smeared with mud and torn in several places. Her cheeks were burned from the biting cold, and her nose was so red she could pass for Rudolph.

She sighed and worked at removing the pins and ties from her hair until it was finally undone, and then used one of the ties to lock it in a bun. The next thing would be to get out of her dress and change into something warm and dry.

Zanya turned to the side and craned her neck as she fumbled with the strings lacing the back of her gown. The damn thing was laced so tight there was no way she could do it herself.

Zanya sighed. Perfect.

She grabbed the dressing room curtain and pulled it aside. "Arwan?"

"Hm?" He lifted his head from his hand where it was rested, his eyes half-glazed over with sleep. Her shoulders slumped forward. The poor guy was exhausted. She couldn't blame him. He'd been through a lot these last few days. They all had.

"I just…" She pointed to her back. "I need some help with this corset thing." The man sitting two chairs to the left of Arwan gawked at her. Zanya made double sure the curtain hid the stain on her dress.

Arwan stood and eased toward her. "Turn around."

She noticed more people shopping and several men slumped in the rows of chairs in the waiting area. "Uh, no. Come inside." There was no way she'd let him undo this thing with everyone around. The fact she had to ask for help undressing was humiliating enough.

He opened the curtain and slipped in, then secured it behind him. He rested his hands on her waist. "Turn around."

She did and stood with her back straight, watching his reflection in the mirror while he worked at loosening her bodice.

The pressure around her ribcage eased, and she drew in a deep breath. "Oh thank God. That thing was killing me."

The air caressed her skin as the damp corset

slowly opened, exposing the curves of her back. She crossed her arms over her chest to prevent the top half of the gown from falling off. The tightly laced ribbon was the only thing holding her top in place.

Arwan worked to unlace the last of the silk ribbon. His fingers brushed against her lower back, spreading warmth up her spine. She studied him in the mirror. He was soaked and miserable, yet he hadn't complained—not even once.

"You should go get changed," she said. "I can handle it from here."

He rested his hands on her shoulders, and his gaze slid over her bare back.

Besides riding together in the taxi, they hadn't spent more than a few moments alone since London. The longing she had carried all this time now overwhelmed her.

He placed a kiss on the curve of her shoulder. Her eyes fluttered shut, and she gripped her dress tighter, tilting her head to the side and exposing her neck.

"Arwan," she whispered. This wasn't really the best place, never mind the fact she probably smelled like wet dog.

He hooked her elbow and gently spun her around. Her heart was no longer hers. It belonged to him completely, and even though they'd only met recently, it seemed as if they'd known each other for a lifetime.

Whatever drew them to each other—whatever made her promise herself to him so completely— they had a bond that would never be broken. Even though the bond had surprised her, she'd made it with all of her heart.

He cradled her face. "If anything happened to you…" His jaw tightened. She wanted to press her fingers against his chest and run her hands along the curves of his shoulders.

He brushed his thumb along her lips, and his eyes flickered to them. *"Si algo te hubiera pasado…me hubiera roto el corazón."*

Her chest tightened. She really, really needed to learn Spanish. But regardless of what he said, hearing him whisper like that made her weak in the knees. Not because of the words, but the way he said them and the heightened intensity of his gaze.

He pulled her close and kissed her, one arm wrapped around her waist, the other caressing her cheek. The light in her chest, the mark of her heritage and power, flickered on and filled her with the cold energy it always brought.

She pried her arms free and wrapped them around his neck. With the top of her gown pinned between their bodies, the sides of the corset fell open, exposing the curves of her waist. He ran his hands along the length of her bare back before settling them on her hips.

The light in her chest brightened, and electricity spread over her skin. His lips curved into a smile, causing her to pause. "Your heart's racing." His gaze flickered to her chest. "I can hear it."

She ran her fingers through his hair and drew him closer, into a kiss. He didn't object but held her with a tenderness he hadn't shown before. Her light dimmed as a new type of passion took over.

She didn't just want him, she wanted his heart,

forever.

"Ahem." A woman on the other side of the curtain cleared her throat, sounding annoyed. Zanya pulled away and looked down. At the bottom of the curtain, she saw the foot of a store employee tapping impatiently. "Is everything all right in there, or do I need to call security?"

Zanya's cheeks blazed with heat.

"Maybe we should finish getting our supplies," Arwan said in a low voice. He faced the curtain with a crooked grin.

Zanya nodded, and he slipped out of the dressing room to speak to the woman waiting outside. His tone was apologetic while he explained Zanya's wardrobe malfunction.

The time is getting closer now, a voice whispered in her mind.

She shut her eyes and tried to block it out. The light in her chest grew warm rather than cold, making her stomach gurgle with a sick heat.

Prepare to rule under me, the voice continued.

Zanya cupped her hands over her ears and squinted her eyes shut.

You are mine. Don't ever believe differently.

The whispers had begun after she'd claimed the ancient Mayan relic and taken it back from Sarian. She suspected this voice was his, reaching through the only link they shared and using one of the few things she loved to drive her mad.

After spending more than she could comprehend at the sporting goods store, Zanya and Arwan loaded all of their new supplies into two hiking packs. With Cualli's pendant hanging around her neck, Zanya unzipped the front pocket and transferred the very last and most important item.

Her stone.

The only pocket big enough to accommodate the large oval stone was the one at the front of the pack. The stone's energy scraped against her skin, raw and sharp from Sarian's partial hold. He may have broken the spell set upon the stone at its creation that made it obey only the guardian, but it still recognized her.

Unfortunately, unlike when she'd bonded with it, her stone no longer spoke to her. It was quiet. Too quiet.

Its colors morphed and pulsed, transforming from its normal hues of white and blue to deep violet and brown. Its polluted energy burned her skin as if she were handling a hot coal. She wanted to flinch away, but ground her teeth and cradled the stone closer. She had to prove it was home, where it belonged. Luckily she could heal after her brief encounters with the stone.

"Are you ready?" Arwan stood and slung his pack over his shoulder.

She rubbed her temples, then blinked to clear her vision.

"What's wrong?"

Zanya shook her head. "Nothing. I just have a headache and…" She considered telling him about the whispers, but that would only worry him. If she got some rest, her mind would be stronger and maybe more capable of fending off the mental attacks. She stood and slipped on her backpack. "Never mind. It's not important. Let's go."

ACKNOWLEDGEMENTS

To my many editors, who all had a hand in making this book shine—thank you. Deranged Doctor Designs, thank you for creating the face of my series in such a breathtaking way. Lastly, thank you for friends and family, who have been endlessly supportive of my writing.

About the Author

A long-time enthusiast of things that go bump in the night, Theresa began her writing career as a journalism intern—possibly the least creative writing field out there. After her first semester at a local newspaper, she washed her hands of press releases and feature articles to delve into the whimsical world of young adult paranormal romance. Since then, Theresa has married, had three terrific kids, and moved to central Ohio where she has been repeatedly guilt tripped into adopting a menagerie of animals that are now members of the family. But don't be fooled by her domesticated appearance. Her greatest love is travel. Having stepped foot on over a dozen countries, and traveled to dozens of U.S. states—including an extended seven-year stay in Kodiak, Alaska—she is anything but settled down. But wherever life brings her, she will continue to weave tales of adventure and love with the hope her stories will bring joy and inspiration to her readers.

Facebook:
https://www.Facebook.com/theresa.dalayne

Twitter:
https://www.twitter.com/theresadalayne

Goodreads:
https://www.goodreads.com/author/show/7847410.
Theresa_DaLayne

Website:
http://TheresaDaLayne.com/

Instagram:
http://www.instagram.com/authortheresadalayne

Mailing List:
http://tinyurl.com/zsgroos

If you enjoyed this book, please take a moment to review it. Your honest feedback means a lot to me. I love hearing from my readers, and I hope you feel free to contact me through any one of my social media sites.

www.ingramcontent.com/pod-product-compliance
Lightning Source LLC
Chambersburg PA
CBHW020526120726
47904CB00003B/982